PRAISE FOI

"If you've never read a Vivian Arend book you are missing out on one of the best contemporary authors writing today."
~ *Book Reading Gals*

"The bitter cold of Alberta, Canada, is made toasty warm by the super-sexy Coleman brothers of Six Pack Ranch."
~ *Publishers Weekly*

"Brilliant, raw, imaginative, irresistible!!"
~ *Avon Romance*

"This story will keep you reading from the first page to the last one. There is never a dull moment..."
~ *Landy Jimenez*

"I definitely recommend to fans of contemporaries with hot cowboys and strong family ties.."
~ *SmexyBooks*

"This was my first Vivian Arend story, and I know I want more! "
~ *Red Hot Plus Blue Reads*

"In this steamy new episode in the "Six Pack Ranch" series, Trevor is a true cowboy hero and will make any reader's heart beat a little faster as he and Becky discover what being a couple is all about."
~ *Library Journal Starred Review*

A FIREFIGHTER'S CHRISTMAS GIFT

HOLIDAYS IN HEART FALLS: BOOK 1

VIVIAN AREND

ALSO BY VIVIAN AREND

Six Pack Ranch

Rocky Mountain Heat

Rocky Mountain Haven

Rocky Mountain Desire

Rocky Mountain Rebel

Rocky Mountain Freedom

Rocky Mountain Romance

Rocky Mountain Retreat

Rocky Mountain Shelter

Rocky Mountain Devil

Rocky Mountain Home

Rocky Mountain Forever

The Stones of Heart Falls

A Rancher's Heart

A Rancher's Song

A Rancher's Bride

A Rancher's Love

A Rancher's Vow

A full list of Vivian's print titles is available on her website

www.vivianarend.com

A Firefighter's Christmas Gift

ISBN: 9781989507254
Edited by Anne Scott
Cover Design © Damonza
Proofed by Angie Ramey & Linda Levy

With great thanks and many hugs to Shannon Stacey. You write the most delightful holiday stories. You inspired me to make that happen for myself. May you always have mischief, mistletoe and happily-ever-afters.

1

There were twelve days until Christmas, which didn't seem like long enough considering everything Hanna Lane needed to accomplish.

Still, some things were meant to be savoured. She wrapped both hands around the cup of mocha latte she'd allowed herself to splurge on, sipping slowly with her eyes closed as she let the sounds in the Buns and Roses coffee shop wrap around her like a warm, winter blanket.

Familiar voices, delicious scents. Tansy Fields's cinnamon buns made Hanna drool just thinking about them. But she wanted to share the treat she'd bought with her daughter Crissy, which meant keeping the top of the paper bag firmly folded to help resist temptation.

Didn't mean Hanna couldn't *pretend* she had all the options from behind the counter for her tasting pleasure.

A chair squeaked, and she popped her eyes open to discover an enormous, broad-chested man settling himself carefully into the wrought-iron chair on the opposite side of the table. Brad Ford's deep blue eyes swept over her, a smile on his face.

"Hey, Hanna."

He reached up and pulled off his toque, running a hand over the short stubble on his head. Hanna couldn't tear her eyes away. It wasn't right how simply looking at him was enough to make her hot and cold at the same time.

He was just so *big*. Big hands, big arms, big biceps being revealed as he shrugged out of his winter coat and draped it over the back of the chair behind him. His long-sleeved T-shirt was living on borrowed time, stretched hard across his shoulders and chest.

A soft cough reached her ears.

Oops, she'd been staring. Hanna's gaze shot back to Brad's face where his smile had twisted toward amusement. "Good afternoon, Hanna. Do you need another coffee?"

"No, thank you. I just started this one."

He moved slowly, the same as usual, but there was so much of him that she always felt like a munchkin when he was around. He settled his elbows on the table in front of him, leaning toward her.

He spoke at the perfect volume so she could hear him but wasn't easily overheard by their neighbours at the nearby tables. "Sorry I had to cancel last night."

Hanna was too, and yet at the same time, maybe she wasn't. "You're a firefighter. You can't help when you're going to get called out."

"But I was looking forward to our date. You don't often have a Tuesday night free, and I know you set up a special babysitter."

Hanna played with her cup. It was easier to not look at him when they spoke, because it still didn't seem possible he was interested in *her*. "It probably turned out for the best, because it was a school night. My sitter said she had a test to study for."

They were interrupted by the arrival of Brad's food. Fern Fields, the youngest of the Fields family, lowered the tray in front of Brad. She glanced between the two of them, her riotous black curls dancing around her head as her expression grew inquisitive. "Can I get you another drink, Hanna?"

"No, thanks," Hanna told her quickly.

"Go ahead and get her a second one, and put it on my bill," Brad insisted over Hanna's protest. "You can take it home and warm it up later if you don't drink it now."

"One dark-chocolate mocha latte, on its way." Fern waited until Brad transferred the plates to the table before she grabbed the tray with her prosthetic hand and headed back to the counter, humming cheerfully as she dodged tables and people.

Hanna tried her best to look stern as she chided Brad, but she was distracted by the sheer amount of food. "You don't need to go buying me things."

"You're right. I don't," he agreed, even as he grabbed a cinnamon bun and put the plate in front of her. "Here. This is for you."

"*Brad.*"

His eyes twinkled. "It's my apology for leaving you dateless last night. Seriously. Otherwise, I'll feel terrible all day."

He *was* terrible. And relentless—and Hanna wasn't quite sure how to deal with him. She looked at the cinnamon bun and up at him, but when her stomach growled and he lifted a brow, there wasn't much she could do in protest. "Thank you."

He nodded happily, picking up his own enormous muffin and taking an enthusiastic bite.

They were quiet for a moment as they both enjoyed their treats, but Hanna wondered again what she was thinking. This man had done everything possible to make it clear he was attracted to her and wanted them to spend time together, but still she hesitated.

She wasn't sure if her concerns were real or caused by ghosts from the past.

Hanna peeled off another bit of cinnamon bun and popped it in her mouth as she covertly peeked in his direction. Someone at a nearby table was talking with him, not as if she were being ignored but as if Brad was giving her a bit of space.

Brad Ford might be a giant, but he was a gentle giant. Only, Hanna had an eight-year-old daughter who was her first priority, and not even the butterflies of attraction were enough to let her risk Crissy being hurt.

His determined pursuit made Hanna uncomfortable in ways she hadn't felt for a long time. She was smart enough to know that they weren't necessarily *wrong* ways, but she still needed to go slowly. Very, *very* slowly.

Brad turned toward her, offering her a muffin, and this time when she shook her head he relented instantly.

They were mostly quiet, sharing a companionable silence as Hanna reached the bottom of her first cup of coffee. She checked the time as she considered what she needed to accomplish before meeting Crissy after school. First on the list was an afternoon nap, because her late-night job cleaning offices meant she could either rest for a while each day or end up like a zombie by the end of the week.

She gathered her things as she glanced across the table at Brad. "Thank you for the lunch treat. I didn't expect it. It was a nice surprise."

His face lit up as if she'd given him some kind of prize. "Glad to do it, sugar. I hope Crissy enjoys the cinnamon bun."

Hanna could picture her daughter's delight at the sweet treat. "I..." Funny how she wanted to stay *and* to escape. "I should go."

"Can I see you later this week? Maybe we should try a date during the day so you don't have to worry about getting a babysitter."

She was more tempted than she should be. It was a generous and observant offer. "Maybe."

He leaned in again, and it seemed as if there were just the two of them in the crowded coffee shop. "Horseback riding?"

Observant and evil. Horses were her kryptonite. She looked him over and, for one brief moment, allowed herself to enjoy the entire beautiful package of manhood. "Tuesday or Wednesday next week?"

"Friday? Or Monday?" As if he was too eager to wait.

Hanna laughed. "Okay, Monday. But I need to be back at the school by three o'clock when Crissy is done. And I can't go until eleven o'clock." Because while she could mess with her schedule a little, like napping before lunch instead of after, she needed to get at least a couple hours of sleep.

He had no arguments. "I'll pick you up, because I don't think your car can make it up the road to our ranch."

A shiver of excitement slid over her, but as she picked up her coffee in one hand and her bag with the cinnamon bun in the other, she offered a smile, fighting against the feeling another date was a dangerous idea. "Okay, I'll see you then."

He was on his feet, turning as she moved. "I can't wait."

Hanna pushed past him, the scent of his soap and the sheer presence of him like a touch. She headed onto the street, her boots sliding in the snow coating the sidewalk as she returned to her and Crissy's apartment. They lived upstairs above the ground floor businesses one street over from Buns and Roses.

As she carefully put her drink and the treat in the fridge then headed off to crawl into bed for a bit, she was a mass of shivers and excitement.

Was it possible for something good to be coming her way?

BRAD CAUGHT himself whistling as he took the steep road to the sprawling ranch house where he'd grown up. Even after being called out on a fire at a most annoying time, and having to stay until nearly two a.m. to make sure there were no lingering sparks from the old barn that had gotten out of control, Brad was pretty much happy as a clam.

He would've been happier had he'd made the date with sweet Hanna Lane, but he was a patient man. He was pretty sure there was no use in pushing to move faster than they were already going.

Brad wasn't stupid. He could tell she was interested, but she was also either incredibly shy or nervous. So be it.

He was patient, but also determined. Coming back to Heart Falls where he'd grown up had been a deliberate choice. Not only so he could be there for his dad, but because he'd enjoyed living in the small town when he was young.

His training as an EMT and firefighter had taken him away, but now he was back, with a good job and enough money in the bank, thanks to an inheritance from when his mom had passed away. He was ready to settle down and raise a family of his own.

Coming back to a small town was a risky proposition in terms of potential relationships, though. There was no way to know who'd still be around, and who'd already found their special someone, which was why he'd been delighted to discover Hanna Lane had moved into the area.

Oh, he'd seen her a couple of times while visiting his father over the years. She had long brown hair she wore loose around her shoulders and big brown eyes that made him want to stare at her for hours. Soft curves on a petite frame—she was spectacular enough to catch his attention but quiet enough he'd never pushed to officially meet her. Not until last June when he'd moved back to town for good.

Ever since then it'd been two steps forward, three steps back in a dating dance. He was serious, but Hanna didn't seem to think he was. Hanna didn't seem to know what she was ready for, and he hadn't pressed her.

They'd had a half-dozen official dates since October, and he'd kissed her twice. Not even real kisses, because once she'd twisted her head and his cautious attempt had landed on her forehead, and the second time he'd hit her cheek. He'd worried that he'd been pushing too hard, but she'd smiled sweetly, and he'd hoped, and...

No matter that he'd been hard and aching for more, he'd been shockingly content to head home each time, determined to go at her pace.

Brad pulled over the ridge of the hill, and the Lone Pine ranch house appeared, the stately wood siding worn by time yet still sturdy. His father had slowed down over the past years, especially after Brad's mom, Connie, had died two years ago.

But Patrick Ford had cared for the place best he could until his accident in early June. Since then, he'd slowly been getting rid of the animals and renting out the fields to neighbours.

Between his social security and the bit of income from the ranch, his father was doing fine financially. Brad had willingly taken over repairs and his share of the expenses. Heck, he was willing to pay them all if necessary.

He just wanted his dad to be happy. Patrick was still weak from a tractor accident, and it was a tough time of year as the anniversary of Connie's death approached.

Patrick losing his life partner of nearly forty years had left him more handicapped in some ways than the damage to his legs from being rolled under the heavy equipment.

Outside the house, his dad's well-worn Chevy truck was parked close to the door. Next to it sat a shiny new Hyundai that looked very out of place in the rustic surroundings. Brad wondered how on earth the vehicle had made it up the snowy drive.

When he pushed through the back door to raised voices, Brad strode in with his boots on, marching through the foyer to the living room.

"Maybe if you'd ever shown that you gave a damn about me, I'd think differently," Patrick Ford said, the silver white hair on his head standing upright as if he'd dragged a hand through it. He glared sternly at Brad's older brother, Mark. "There's no use in arguing. I've made up my mind."

"What's going on?" Brad interrupted. "Mark, what are you doing here?"

His brother turned on him, anger in his eyes. He wasn't as big overall as Brad, built more along the lean, narrow lines he'd inherited from their mother. "It's my house too. I have every right to be here."

"You're welcome to visit, but it's *not* your house," their dad said firmly, leaning back in his easy chair as if there weren't raised voices echoing off the walls.

"Mark. Dad." Brad stepped between the two of them, putting his hand on his brother's chest. Mark was nearly vibrating with anger. "I didn't mean *what are you doing here* like you're not allowed, I just didn't expect you. What's going on? And don't shout, my hearing is fine."

Mark stepped back, pacing the room, the worn wooden flooring letting out a protest, each footfall echoing with a staccato crunch. "He told me to come. Said he had something to tell us, but what he really meant was he wanted me here so he could spit in my face."

Brad took a deep breath and fought for strength. His dad and his older brother had a falling out years ago, and while he'd tried to convince them to move on, neither of them would budge an inch. It had only gotten worse after Connie died.

Brad put as much authority into his tone as possible, snapping a finger at the chair in the opposite corner from where his dad sat. "Mark, sit down and we'll figure this out."

To his shock, his brother actually cooperated, dropping into the chair then glaring at Patrick.

Brad focused on his father. "Dad? Did you ask Mark to come?"

Patrick nodded. "I didn't mean to tell him anything until you were here as well. But he makes me so damn angry—"

"*I* make you angry? You should try living with yourself, old man. You're the most—"

"Be quiet," Brad roared, his voice echoing off the walls. "Both of you."

The two of them quelled, stubborn anger painting their features, but at least now their mouths were shut.

What a mixed-up day. What a change of emotion, to go from daydreaming about sweet Hanna to having to deal with his family's inflammatory situation. "I don't have the time or patience to deal with this if all you're going to do is shout at each other. Mark, stop interrupting and let Dad have his say. But Dad, you can talk without insulting anyone."

Patrick broke off his staring match with his elder son to meet Brad's gaze. "I'm just taking care of my estate. Doing the things your mother and I discussed when she was still alive. Damn if I want the tax department to get fifty percent of everything we worked to build."

"You're far from being dead," Brad pointed out, "and to be blunt, when you're gone, it won't be your problem. Mark and I will deal with it."

"The same way he dealt with the money Connie left him? Let it run through his fingers like it was water?"

Mark made a sound as if he was going to speak then locked his jaw together, fists tightening on the arms of the chair.

Patrick looked up at Brad. "Of course I'm dying."

Brad felt his legs go weak, and he dropped onto the couch. "*What?* What's wrong?"

His father had the grace to look guilty. "No. I don't mean that. Just that we're *all* dying. And my accident proved we never know when life might change. Now with my damn legs, and—"

"Jeez, Dad, don't scare the hell out of us like that." Brad glanced at his brother in the hopes their father's moment of vulnerably had broken through his hard shell.

Mark was still glaring. It seemed his brother's heart truly was a rock.

Patrick cleared his throat then spoke firmly. "It was my choice. I sent a letter to my lawyer to get things set up, so it's done. I told him I was giving it all to you, Brad. Which means I'm now officially your responsibility, but *you* I trust. I know you won't kick me out on my ass or put me in some old-age home and never come and see me."

"This is my home too. You can't just give everything to Brad," Mark snapped. "You're out of your goddamn mind."

His father raised a brow, but instead of shouting, he spoke more softly. "And maybe that right there is an answer to why I trust Brad to take care of me, and not you."

"So just like that, you'll cut me out of everything?"

"It's done," Patrick said.

Brad sighed. "I wish you'd talked to me about this first, Dad. I mean it's your decision what you do with your money and the house—"

"Of course, you'd say that, since you're getting everything," Mark snapped, rising to his feet. He glared between the two of them. "You haven't heard the last of this. You just can't up and give everything to him."

All the shout seemed to have left his father. Patrick stared sadly at his oldest son. "There's nothing you can do to change my mind about that part. You've spent the last five years showing how little you respect me, the ranch, your mother when she was still alive. I don't trust you right now. So whatever debts you built up that you were hoping for your inheritance to clear up, you'll just have to grow a pair and get yourself out of trouble on your own. You made your choices, son. Now you have to live with them."

It was softly spoken, but sharp as a knife.

"So. That's it?"

"I guess it is."

Mark stomped from the room, slamming the door behind him. In the quiet that fell, an engine raced before fading into the distance.

Patrick looked pale. Brad went over to kneel by his Dad's feet, taking his hand and covertly checking his pulse.

His father shook his head. "I'm sorry that turned out so harsh."

"Me too." Brad sat back on the coffee table, keeping hold of his dad's hand. "We're not done talking. I meant it—it's your decision to do what you want with the ranch. And you're right. Mark needs to take responsibility and grow up. But I don't think it's a good idea to close the door on him. He's still your son and my brother. People can change."

Patrick's silvery-white head dipped slowly. "I know. It's hard to see the big picture when I'm running on piss and vinegar. Connie wouldn't be very happy with me right now." He sighed heavily. "I should have talked to you first."

"You should have, but we'll do what we can to move forward. How about we give Mark a bit of time to cool off, then send him an email," Brad suggested. "Tell him to come visit. It would be nice to start being a family again someday."

Patrick stared off into space. "Damn, I miss your mom. She

wouldn't have been able to fix this, but just talking to her always made the burden lighter."

Brad knew what his dad was talking about better than he'd ever imagined, because in the space of a few months, everything had changed.

The strongest longing inside him was to go find Hanna and pull her against him. To hold her tight as he shared what had just happened. He wanted to let her into his world and let her support him.

It was something to be thought about...

2

Friday night Crissy crawled onto Hanna's lap, homework reading book at the ready. "What time do you have to leave for work, Mommy?"

"Soon. Mrs. Nonnie should be here anytime."

Her little girl snuggled in tight then turned the pages slowly, reading the words with care. Hanna prompted her when necessary, but for the most part she just soaked in the warmth of her precious child.

Every moment of struggle up to this point had been worth it because of Crissy. Every relationship that she'd had to turn her back on, Hanna couldn't regret any of them because Crissy was here and happy, and thriving as much as she could.

There were sad truths. Crissy didn't have a grandma and grandpa because when Hanna had found out she was pregnant, the first thing her parents had done after looking at her with horror and shock was to tell her to pack a bag and get out.

Hanna pushed the memory away. Those were nightmare thoughts and not something she wanted in her life. She focused on Crissy, who smiled up at her after sounding out an exceptionally hard word.

"That says beautiful," Crissy informed her.

"It does. Well done."

Crissy lifted a hand to touch her cheek. "I think you're beautiful."

Hanna's heart filled. "Thank you. I think you're beautiful too."

The phone rang, and Hanna picked it up.

"Hanna, honey. I'm sorry, but there's no way I can come over." Something in Mrs. Nonnie's throat made a horrible sizzling sound, and the woman paused to blow her nose before coming back to finish in a hoarse whisper. "I should have called earlier, but I fell asleep."

This night was going from bad to worse. "I'm sorry you're not feeling well. Of course, you should stay home and get better."

"You take care."

Even as Hanna hung up, she scolded herself for not realizing this could happen. Mrs. Nonnie had cancelled only a few nights ago, and Hanna had been forced to scramble and drop Crissy off with friends.

While Hanna had booked a different sitter for her and Brad's cancelled date, getting a teenager at the last minute on a Friday night was out of the question.

She checked the time. It was too late to ask her friends for help.

Crissy took a deep breath. "I'm big enough to stay home by myself," she said in a soft whisper.

"Oh, darling. No, you're not. I'm sorry, but you're going to have to come with Mommy. We'll bring your sleeping bag, and you can have a camping trip, okay?"

It was going to make everything harder, but what choice did

she have? And it wasn't something that she hadn't had to do at different times over the years.

Crissy headed off to gather her things.

"Don't put on pyjamas. Wear your soft sweatpants and blue hoodie," Hanna reminded her.

Most of her cleaning supplies were already in the car. Hanna grabbed the basket of things she brought in every day to keep them from freezing, then packed a snack and a bottle of water for Crissy. She added a couple of books and a flashlight to turn it into a camping adventure.

It took an extra trip to get from the car into the office, and it took time to set up Crissy in her "tent", but as Hanna went about cleaning the accounting firm that was her first of four jobs for the night, it was a little like stepping back in time.

After Crissy had been born, Hanna had needed a job. She'd worked for another woman for a year, sharing an apartment with two single moms. They'd arranged their schedules so they could babysit in a rotation.

When that had fallen apart, though, Hanna had come to Heart Falls. She'd started out by bringing in a portable playpen for Crissy to sleep and play in, and when that didn't work, she had a backpack she wore, the motion of moving back and forth with the vacuum cleaner and the rest of her tasks were enough to put a tired toddler to sleep.

Every job had taken a little longer, but it made it possible for Hanna to bring in enough work to pay the bills.

The fact that Crissy was a beautiful, sweet child made it easier, then, and now. But by the time the third office was done it was after midnight, and Hanna began to feel the extra effort it had taken to get through her tasks.

She carried a sleeping Crissy upstairs back to their apartment and laid her in bed. This she would allow herself to do. The final office that needed to be cleaned was the law firm directly below their home. And with the baby monitor turned on, if Crissy did need her, Hanna could be upstairs in under a minute.

She pressed a kiss to her sleeping daughter's forehead. "Mommy loves you," she whispered.

Crissy's arms came up and tangled around her neck, squeezing tight. "I love you, Mommy. This is my bed," she said drowsily.

"Yes. Your camping trip is over. Mommy has to go downstairs to finish work, but if you need me, just call out, okay? I've got the special telephone with me."

"Okay." Crissy was asleep before she finished rolling over.

It was tough work to do the last office. Probably because Hanna's afternoon nap had been more tossing and turning than sleeping, images of Brad interrupting her far too often.

She needed to figure out what she was doing with the man. It wasn't fair to keep going out with him if she wasn't interested in getting serious.

On the other hand, she couldn't decide if she was interested unless she knew he truly was serious. He seemed to be, and he was persistent, but it was pretty clear she didn't have a very good handle on when guys were serious and when they were just trying to get something. And by get something, she meant sex.

The back kitchen area of the law office looked as if someone had held a party before an earthquake struck. And when Hanna went to move the coffee maker and it tipped, cold coffee spilling everywhere, it just added to the disaster.

By the time the room was sparkling, she was tired enough she had to sit down. She laid her head on her arms and closed her eyes for a moment.

She probably could've gotten away with a little less work, but Mr. Boise had been kind to her right from the start when she'd arrived in Heart Falls. He'd been the first to hire her, and offered a recommendation so she'd gotten into the apartment above his office.

He'd also helped her do up the paperwork necessary to make sure no one could ever take Crissy from her. Not that she expected the sperm donor to show up asking for parental rights, but she wasn't taking any chances.

She could see Crissy's clear grey eyes looking at her with trust. Hanna dreamed of taking her somewhere pretty, up on a mountainside, with a swing set and maybe some horses—Crissy loved horses as much as Hanna had at that age.

A loud buzzing filled her ears, and Hanna realized she'd fallen asleep at the table. She looked up in shock to discover the room was filled with smoke, and the buzzer was a fire alarm going off.

Crissy.

Hanna leapt to her feet, racing down the hall toward the front door.

She jerked to a stop in the doorway as heat slammed into her face. The entire front office was filled with flames, and she turned, darting to the back entrance, frantically patting her pockets for her phone as she ran.

She hit 911 even as she put her shoulder to the emergency exit and another alarm rang out.

Hanna raced to the entrance leading to the stairs to the apartments before she discovered her keys were back in the law office. She was in the back alley in nothing but her T-shirt and jeans, her purse and jacket left on the table beside the rest of her things.

"*No.*" She pounded on the door, desperate for Crissy to hear.

"Nine-one-one, what's the nature of your emergency?"

"There's a fire in the law office, and my little girl is upstairs, and I can't get in. Please, *please,* somebody help me."

BRAD HAD BEEN DOWN at the fire hall when the call came in, the initial warning rising from the switchboard linked to the alarm system from the law office. By the time 911 received the second call, he and the first of the volunteer fire department were headed out in the truck.

It didn't register until he actually saw the building that this was where Hanna lived. Icy fear crawled up his spine, but he moved in well-practiced precision with the other members of his team, sliding into place at the front of the building and hauling out the hoses to deal with the immediate flames.

He shouted orders at his men then took the route around to the back, circling to look for other entrances.

He found Hanna pounding on a closed, locked door, screaming at the top of her lungs.

"Someone get me a blanket," he shouted back at the lookout at the corner before examining her quickly. He scanned her hands and arms, running a hand over her head. "Are you okay? Were you in the fire?"

"Crissy. *Crissy* is upstairs," she said, trying to get past him and back to the door.

His heart fell all the way down to his toes. He gripped Hanna by the shoulders and leaned over to look her in the eye. "I'll go get her. You stay here."

Hanna shook her head frantically. "I know where she is."

"Tell me. Back bedroom or front?" He knew the layout of the place from years ago, but he also knew that in a fire, kids didn't stay where they started.

Another EMT had showed up, wrapping a blanket around Hanna's shoulders.

She tried to push it off, tears shining in her eyes but anger there too. "I have to save her," she shouted.

The crew had the door open, and Brad couldn't wait any longer.

"See that she stays here," he ordered the EMT before bending down and grabbing hold of her, looking her square in the eyes. "Hanna, I'm going to get Crissy for you. You *have* to stay here."

He squeezed her briefly, and she nodded, expression sharpening as she remembered something. "Her secret code is Santa Claus. She might not come with you willingly without it."

"Got it." He carefully forced her back into the protective arms of a volunteer. Then he whirled, pulling down his face mask and motioning for his partner to join him as they entered the smoke-filled stairwell.

The heavy weight of his equipment didn't exist as he sprinted upward, pivoting on the landing toward Hanna's apartment. He and Mack checked both doors quickly.

Mack swore as he pulled away from the empty apartment. "She's got a backdraft building."

"This one is still cool," Brad told him. One solid kick at the lock level was enough to send wood splintering.

At some other time he'd have worried about how flimsy the protection guarding Hanna and Crissy was, but right now, he was glad.

"Crissy. It's Mommy's friend, Brad. We're here to help you." The shout came out garbled by his mask, and Brad cursed softly before lifting it partway, directing Mack toward the front bedroom. "Crissy, we have to get out of the apartment. Hanna said you need to come with us."

Smoke was pumping up through the baseboards and registers, the sound of sirens and fire alarms carrying over the fainter but growing crackle of flames. All too familiar, all too dangerous.

Brad slipped into what was definitely a little girl's room, a pretty purple with unicorns and fairytale-creature posters covering the walls. Only the princess palace was rapidly turning into a scene from hell as the fire on the first level took hold of the floor under this part of the building. Walls were buckling with heat, and the surface beneath him creaked ominously.

"Crissy?"

She wasn't in bed, under the bed or in the closet, all the usual places for a frightened child to hide. He checked the toy chest, but there wasn't anywhere else big enough for a kid, not even a slight eight-year-old.

"Other bedroom is empty too," Mack shouted. "Crissy, your mom is waiting for you downstairs. You gotta come with us now."

Heat was rising. The bathroom was a dead end, the kitchen small enough it only took ten seconds to open all the cupboards and peer in them.

Brad shouted Crissy's name again while Mack worked the edge of the living space, running his hand over blankets and curtains, tossing pillows aside. Visibility was fading, the old building giving up as the flames took their toll on wood and insulation, lighting up even as water pounded against the closed windows.

She had to be there.

His gaze fell on the coffee table in the corner. A small artificial Christmas tree rested on top, bare branches like a Charlie Brown tribute.

But the base was covered with a cheery Christmas-coloured cloth that hung all the way to the floor. It would have kept out the worst of the smoke, and been a lot safer than her bedroom.

Was it possible?

A crash sounded from out in the hall. Mack shouted a warning. "Two minutes, tops. Move it, bro."

Brad dropped to his knees and lifted the edge of the fabric, looking into two big grey eyes and the tear-stained face of a mini-

Hanna. "Hey, Crissy. Mommy says Santa Claus wants you to come with me. Okay?"

If he had to, he'd scoop her out of there in under two seconds, but when she immediately crawled forward and threw herself into his arms, he was relieved to avoid adding to what was already a traumatic experience.

He spun. "Got her, Mack. Let's get out of here."

His feet were already moving as he pulled a blanket off the couch. "Crissy, I need you to hide under this for a minute, okay? I'm taking you to your mom."

She clutched him tighter, pressing her face to his chest as he threw the blanket over her head and ducked low, sprinting toward the door where Mack was waiting. His hand caught hold of Brad's gear and shoved him in the right direction.

The stairs were on fire.

Brad jumped the final five steps, one hand on the railing to guide his forward flight, the other holding Crissy against him. They shot out of the door like they were jet propelled, a horrid crashing sound echoing on his heels.

Mack wrapped an arm around Brad's shoulders and together they rushed to the safe zone. Behind them the fire protested their escape, an eardrum-rattling shriek echoing as the building gave up.

He glanced back, and the blanket over Crissy's head shifted as she wiggled upright. Haunted little-girl eyes took in the flames and crashing walls, heat roiling over them.

She turned her gaze upward as he hurried to the ambulance where Hanna was being forcibly restrained to keep her from rushing them. "You're okay, sweetie," he assured her. "And Mommy is right here. Let's be brave for her, okay?"

Crissy pressed her lips tight, but her head dipped the tiniest bit.

"You hug your mama, but then we have to let my friends take

a look to be sure the smoke didn't get inside you. Can you do that?"

Hanna had broken free and was closing the distance between them, the spare jacket someone had given her hanging nearly to her knees.

Brad gave Mack a nod. "Take over. I need a second."

"No prob." His second-in-command slapped his shoulder briefly before raising an arm and shouting orders, the volunteer crew rushing to fill him in. They dragged in extra hoses, but at this point Brad doubted they could keep the other buildings on the street from going up as well.

His attention went to Hanna, bending his knees far enough he could open his arm and let her catch hold of Crissy without taking the little girl fully from him.

"Is she okay? Are you okay—?"

"She's good," Brad assured her quickly. "She came right away when I told her to, and she's not hurt."

"Oh my god, baby. Mommy's so sorry. I'm so sorry." Hanna dropped kisses over her daughter's face, leaning in and pressing their foreheads together. "I love you."

"Love you, Mommy." Crissy snuck a hand out and wiped at a tear on Hanna's cheek. "Santa Claus told me to hide."

"I'm glad—"

"Hanna, we need to go back to the ambulance," Brad interrupted. "Come on."

He curled his arm around her and guided her toward the emergency vehicle, the strangest sensation growing in his belly.

Post-rescue adrenaline always left a buzz, but this was more. Something tangled and powerful. Seeing the sheer relief on Hanna's face was compounded by the grip her daughter had on his neck. Crissy had wiggled one arm around him and was clinging like a monkey.

When they reached the truck and he tried to lower Crissy to the gurney, she refused to let go.

Hanna had Crissy by one hand, but the other had slipped down to tangle in the loops of his jacket.

Brad closed his fingers over hers. "Hey, kiddo. I told you about this. You need to let the doctors peek at you."

She tugged again. "Stay."

"Crissy, Brad has to work still. Mommy will stay with you."

Crissy's eyes were fixed on Brad. "Come back?"

"I'll be back when I can," he promised. "Be good for your mommy and help the EMT." He tapped her nose gently with a gloved finger, sliding his gaze over Hanna.

She stood ramrod straight, watching like a mama bear as the EMT moved in to start the examination. Everything she owned was burning to the ground behind them, but she didn't seem to care. All her attention was on Crissy.

Brad forced himself to step away. There were decisions he needed to make.

Behind him, Hanna's voice rose, clear and comforting. The voice of an angel, not a woman on the brink of a breakdown. "Everything will be okay, sweetie. Everything will be okay."

Leaving nearly killed him, but that moment was enough to make one thing very clear. Everything *was* going to be okay, because he would do whatever it took to be sure that was true for Hanna and Crissy in the future.

Whatever it took.

3

It was three a.m., and Hanna was dead on her feet. She was bundled up on the edge of a truck bumper, wrapped in so many blankets she felt like a mummy. Crissy had been given a clean bill of health, but it'd taken extra time because they'd had to shift the entire operation halfway down the block.

The entire row of shops was burning, structural walls collapsing.

Hanna had stood helplessly by as a portion of the old red-stone building had given way, crumbling southward with a crashing rush to cover her car with bricks and debris. Everything was gone, including her phone which had become a victim of the evening as well when it slipped from her fingers during the crisis and been crushed underfoot.

In her lap, Crissy slept like the innocent she was, content to be in her mama's arms. Although, until her eyes had reluctantly closed, she'd been watching closely for any sign that *her* fireman was coming back.

And now that Crissy was asleep, Hanna found she couldn't take her eyes off the man.

He seemed to be in more than one place at the same time, moving quickly back and forth, his heavy equipment not slowing him down in the least.

The EMT was back, looking at her with concern. "You warm enough?"

Out of nowhere, Brad appeared, his mask pushed back, soot smearing his face. "What's going on, Tyler? Why is Hanna still here?"

The man glanced at Hanna before stepping away, and though he spoke quietly, his words carried to her ears. "There's trouble with space at the emergency shelter. And the local motel is completely filled with that bridge-repair team. She called a friend, so she's got a place to stay for the night out at Silver Stone, but her ride hasn't arrived yet."

Brad nodded, turning back to Hanna. "You hanging in there?"

"I'm doing—" Another crash sounded behind him, and she cringed involuntarily. She straightened her spine, looking him in the eye and admitting honestly, "I'm tired, but happy we're safe. Thank you again for saving Crissy."

"She's a smart little thing. You're spending the night with the Stone family?"

She had hated to phone so late, but it was the only place she could think of where Crissy would be comfortable to wake up in the morning. "They should be here soon."

He looked as if he was about to say something else then his name was called, and with a farewell nod he backed away. "Tell Crissy I'll come see her soon."

"Hanna." A shout echoed from the other direction as Caleb Stone marched forward. The familiar face of her friend's husband gave her something new to focus on instead of Brad marching back into the danger zone.

Although, she had to admit she was still watching.

"Let me take Crissy," Caleb said, his voice a low rumble. "We'll get you home and warmed up."

They were both quiet on the drive. At the house a sleepy and green-looking Tamara, moving slowly, offered Hanna a set of pyjamas and a towel. "There's a guest bed in the playroom downstairs. You can keep Crissy with you, or if you want to put her in bed with Emma, that's fine too."

"We're all smoky—"

"If you want to shower, take one, but don't worry about it if you don't want to wake her. Everything is washable."

In the end, Caleb carried Crissy downstairs and laid her on the hide-a-bed. Hanna looked down at her sleeping child for a long time before stepping into the shower and letting the hot water pour over her.

It seemed as if she was never going to get warm.

Morning came far too early, and Hanna opened her eyes to discover she was being watched by a curly-haired blonde with big blue eyes who was perched on the edge of the couch armrest. Emma Stone, one of Crissy's best friends.

"Good morning," Hanna said quietly.

Emma glanced at Crissy, who was wiggling slightly as she cuddled against Hanna's side. "You came for a sleepover?"

Hanna guessed that was one way to put it. "Sort of?"

Crissy was sitting up now, looking at her friend seriously. "Everything got burnt up, but Santa told me what to do."

"Santa talked to you?" Emma crawled onto the bed unselfconsciously, sitting down opposite Crissy as if she had nothing else in the world to do but discuss this in greater detail.

Hanna slipped from the bed while the girls continued to talk, looking at her smoke-scented clothing with dismay.

The second little girl of the household, Sasha, appeared at the top of the stairs. She had a robe in her hands as she marched down and looked Hanna over with far more authority than any ten-year-old should. "Mommy says you can wear this and come upstairs."

"Thank you."

Only it wasn't Tamara who greeted her in the kitchen but her sister Lisa. Hanna had only met the dark-haired woman a few times in passing.

"How are you doing this morning?" Lisa asked.

She lifted a pot of coffee, and Hanna nodded, tugging the front of the robe around herself a little tighter. "I'm alive."

Lisa put down the coffee and came around the island. She held out her arms out wide. "I know I'm not Tamara, but if you need one, she taught me everything I know about hugs."

A shaky laugh escaped as Hanna stepped forward and allowed herself to be enfolded in a tight, giving squeeze. "Thanks."

The other woman gave her an extra pat on the back before releasing her and heading back to the stove. "I put a call out to get you some clothes. Tamara and I would offer you ours, but you'd swim in them. Kelli James who works here is more your size. She said she'd bring over some stuff to tide you over. And between Sasha and Emma, we'll find things for Crissy."

Hanna focused down on her coffee mug, the tightness in her throat growing. She took a deep breath then lifted her eyes with a nod. "I really appreciate it."

"No problem." Lisa got busy at the stove. "Tamara will be up in a little while. This pregnancy is knocking her for a loop, so she tries to avoid moving until after we finish with food and drink."

Lisa ordered Hanna to take her cup and sit by the fire, and Hanna didn't have the strength to argue. She ignored the chairs and settled on the ground in front of the flames, considering how big of a difference it was to have this warmth and comfort compared to the all-encompassing terror of the previous night.

One thing was for sure; she couldn't take advantage of her friends by staying out at Silver Stone for too long.

That decision was made even clearer when Tamara made her way into the room an hour or so later, ghastly white as she moved gingerly to a chair and nibbled on crackers.

"Sorry for not being more help," Tamara apologized. "I will never make fun of anyone with morning sickness ever again."

"I had it pretty bad for the first three months with Crissy," Hanna shared.

"I'm in my second trimester, and if anything, it's gotten worse." Tamara gave her a sheepish smile. "But hey, building babies takes work."

"It's worth it," Hanna agreed.

Since it was Saturday and they had nowhere they needed to take the girls, it had turned into a kind of a sleepover. Crissy settled in with Sasha and Emma and found a couple of outfits to borrow. The offered loaners came in for Hanna, and she had another shower before pulling on well-worn jeans that fit, but didn't.

It was just after lunch when Tamara pulled herself to vertical and offered Hanna a ride into town to see her apartment. "I'm feeling good enough to go with you. You can leave Crissy here."

"I've got the girls," Lisa promised.

Which was a good thing, because the scene wasn't anything Hanna wanted her daughter exposed to that soon.

The flames had been replaced by a smoldering pile of blackened debris and support pillars. Icicles dripped from the rubble like twisted modern art. Even the beauty of frost and ice couldn't make the destruction into something less horrifying than the reality.

There was nothing left.

Tamara wrapped an arm around her. "I'm sorry."

"Me too." Hanna looked down at the ground. At the

running shoes that were her only pair of footwear. Borrowed pants, a borrowed coat. She really did have nothing to her name.

But she had Crissy, and she was more than enough.

She lifted her chin determinedly. She'd started with nothing, and while it hurt to think about how much work it would be to do it again, she could do this.

She turned to Tamara and attempted a smile. "Thank you for taking us in last night."

"You're welcome to stay as long as you need to," Tamara offered. "We'll just have to juggle things a bit."

Hanna nodded. "Can you take me by the fire hall? The EMT last night said I should stop in because emergency services would have information for me."

They returned to the truck but Tamara paused, leaning her head against the window. "Sorry. I think you need to drive."

It was a bit of a stretch, but after adjusting the seat and sitting up as straight as possible, Hanna could both reach the pedals and see out the front window. She drove slowly to the fire hall, trying to avoid the bumps in the road as Tamara gritted her teeth and attempted to put on a happy face.

"Stay here," Hanna offered. "I won't be long."

She hurried into the office of the fire hall.

Brad had made it into work an hour earlier after checking the fire site. They'd hung markers around the territory to keep snoopy parties out, but there wasn't much left to poke through.

He wished he'd grabbed more from the apartment when he'd had a chance, but that was wasted regret. Crissy was alive, and so was Hanna. That's all that mattered.

He was picturing Hanna's face when the door opened and

suddenly she was there, looking a little lost and confused, neither of which he blamed her for.

"Hanna."

Her head swiveled his direction, wide brown eyes that he'd been dreaming about far too often focusing on him with intent. A strange sort of smile twisted her lips, and she met him in the middle of the room and, without any hesitation, wrapped her arms around him and squeezed.

He didn't quite know what to do with his hands. What he wanted to do was hug her back just as tightly, but instead he patted her gently, making sure she could get away when she wanted to. "How are you this morning? How's Crissy?"

Hanna slipped back as if surprised by her boldness, cheeks flushed. "I don't think it's registered yet. She's having a sleepover, and that's the most important thing in her world."

Brad nodded. "I hope that's how it continues, but if she needs some help, or if you do, we've got contact numbers for people who are good to talk to after a loss."

She seemed distracted. "The EMT said there were emergency services I could access. I have tenant insurance, but I don't know how long it'll take to get some money. And I need somewhere to stay."

He headed toward the drawer where the information was kept even as he asked, "I thought you went to Silver Stone?"

Hanna met his gaze, and that steely determination he'd seen before was back. "They're good friends, and they've offered to help us, but I can't stay there for more than a couple of nights."

He pushed the sheet forward, wondering what the problem was.

Something must've shown on his face because Hanna shook her head. "They want me to stay, but Tamara's pregnant, and she's got morning sickness twenty-four hours a day. I can't add two extra house guests to that stress."

"*Ahhh.*"

He glanced at the page under his fingers which offered information about the women's shelter. The nearest one was in Black Diamond, a forty-five-minute drive away. He thought through what he knew of Hanna's friends, and he was sure there was someone local who could offer a temporary place.

Which was why it was to their mutual shock when the next words that came out of his mouth, unplanned but totally perfect, were, "You're welcome to stay with me."

Her eyes widened to the size of dinner plates.

He hurried on to correct himself and explain. "I mean, with my father and I. The house at Lone Pine ranch has a half-dozen rooms, and there's just the two of us. There's no reason why you can't use a couple of them, and to be honest"—he thought quickly, trying to find an excuse that would tempt her—"it would be a really big help."

Hanna's mouth opened and closed, but no words came out.

Which was fine, because it seemed as if Brad suddenly had more than enough words for them both. "My dad's been out of sorts lately, and it would be good to have some company around during the holidays. My mom died two years ago on Christmas Day, and he misses her. Having you and Crissy around would be good for him. Heck, Patrick would probably love to babysit while you work."

Rambling. He was totally rambling. But again, he didn't care as long as he figured out some way to put a smile back on her face. The reality was she'd lost everything, and it didn't make sense for her to be smiling, but it was killing him to see her like this.

The phone rang and Brad had to answer it, which meant if Hanna was going to bolt for the door this would be the perfect time.

Only when he finished answering the question about Christmas bonfire permits and returned to the desk, she was still there. She'd picked up the paper he'd left for her with emergency contact information, her nose wrinkling in an adorable manner.

"Women's shelter. That's for women who've been abused." She shook her head. "We can't stay there. We can't take room from someone whose life might depend on it."

"It's for anyone who needs it," he pointed out reluctantly.

She was frowning now, determination coming back into play. "Your father volunteers at Crissy's school."

Brad nodded. It was one of the things Patrick had begun to do over the past five years as he slowed down work on the ranch. "He said it's a lot more comfortable working in a warm schoolroom than a cold barn."

Hanna stared into his face. "I know him. I've met him a number of times when I've helped in the classroom. Do you really think he wouldn't mind acting as a babysitter for Crissy when I have to work in the evening?"

Holy cow, she was actually considering his offer. "We should ask him."

"Because I don't want to have to take Crissy into town with me, and I don't think that Mrs. Nonnie will drive out to the country." Her steady gaze fluttered away, her cheeks turning brighter red. "But if we do this, just because we're in the same house... *If* I take your offer, that doesn't mean—" She swallowed hard. "I'm not going to— I mean, I know we were kind of trying to date, but—"

"Oh, no. This isn't— I mean—" Damn, he was just about as tongue-tied as she was. He cleared his throat then waited until her gaze rose to meet his. "We *are* dating, but I promise nothing will happen beyond what lines you draw. That means if you move in and we don't do anything more than share a table sometimes, or watch a show with Crissy and my dad, then that's all that happens while you're under my roof."

Although he wanted more, this was not the time and

definitely not the place. But everything in him screamed to offer this bit of protection and comfort, especially heading into the holiday season.

Her head tilted slightly, and Hanna examined him as if she were checking Santa's naughty-and-nice list to see where his name had landed.

After a pause that seemed to last for an eternity, Hanna spoke. "You have to let me help with the cooking."

"All you want," he said with a soft tease. "Especially if your cooking produces some Christmas goodies. I'll buy the ingredients if you provide the manpower."

A flash of her sweet smile returned. "Sweet tooth?"

He nodded. "I can't seem to get enough of sweet things."

He was staring at her a little too hard when he said it, and her cheeks flushed, but she didn't run away.

"We should ask your dad first, about the babysitting."

If he had to pay his dad to make sure he agreed, Hanna and Crissy were going to become their houseguests, come hell or high water. "I'll give him a call then let you know."

She smiled wryly. "Can you do that right now? Because I don't have a working cell phone at the moment. I can wait."

He punched in his dad's number and quickly explained the situation. Patrick, of course, said it wasn't going to be a problem, and suggested Hanna and Crissy should join them for supper.

The relief on her face was clear when Brad shared the news. "That'll give me time to get our things together."

She wrinkled her nose and grimaced, probably realizing it was going to take her all of five minutes to do that.

He worked on offering a steady, reassuring pat on the shoulder. "Then we'll see you this evening. If you can get Caleb Stone to drop you off after five, I'll be there and can show you around."

She left, the snowflakes that swirled in the door after her

melting the instant they hit the ground. Brad stared out the window as she climbed up into an oversized pickup and carefully drove away.

It was nine days until Christmas, and Hanna Lane was moving in with him.

4

It didn't take too much to convince Tamara of the change in accommodation, which was an acknowledgement in itself that Hanna had made the right choice.

While Hanna drove the truck carefully back to Silver Stone, Tamara leaned her face against the cool window and looked miserable. "I'm sorry. I'm being a terrible friend."

"Don't be silly. It's bad enough to be sick. You don't need to feel guilty on top of it." Hanna thought of something. "I do have a favour to ask, other than the things you're already doing, like lending us clothes."

"Anything. Well, anything except dancing a jig or cooking onions," Tamara joked.

It was hard to ask for help, but there was no way around it. Hanna couldn't afford to rent a vehicle, and living out in the country meant she couldn't walk to her jobsites. "Is there a spare vehicle on the ranch I can borrow for a short time? Mine is going to be in the shop for a while getting body work done."

"Of course. We'll ask Caleb, and he'll get you set up." Tamara glanced across at her, a sad smile on her lips. "You really didn't catch much of a break, did you?"

"We made it out alive." It was the most important thing, and Hanna was going to focus on it.

Back at Silver Stone, the girls had made a huge blanket fort, draping fabric over the couch and strategically positioned pillows. Crissy came when Hanna called her, though, Emma at her side, their fingers clasped together.

"Have you had fun playing?" Hanna asked.

Crissy nodded. "Emma's Auntie Lisa made us grilled cheese sandwiches and tomato soup for lunch."

"Sounds yummy." She caught Crissy's free hand. "Mommy found us somewhere to stay for the next little while until we find a new house."

Emma frowned. "I want Crissy to stay with me."

Hanna went to reassure her that they would visit lots, but it was Crissy who spoke up. "Santa Claus said he was going to take care of me, remember?"

Confusion filtered in, at least on Hanna's part.

Emma's face lit up, though, as if she'd completely understood what was going on. "Okay. You want to borrow a stuffie? You can't have Professor G because he would miss me, but you can have someone else come sleep over with you."

Without another word of complaint, Crissy and Emma raced from the room to find Crissy a friend to borrow.

Hanna wandered into the kitchen feeling a little as if she'd been hit by a truck. Tamara had vanished into her bedroom to lie down, profuse apologies spilling from her lips until Hanna had given her a dirty look and sent her from the room.

Lisa put a plate of food in front of Hanna. "I hear you found somewhere to stay?"

"One of the—" Hanna paused. Okay, this was going to be more awkward than she'd imagined. She stuck to basic information. "One of the firefighters has extra space, so we're going to stay there until we figure out the next thing to do."

Lisa settled on the stool beside her. "I know Tamara would love to have you here if she were feeling better, but her pregnancy isn't cooperating. I'm here to help take up the slack, so I stole the guest room. With the holidays, we've got other family coming to visit over the next couple weeks."

"Don't you apologize, either." Hanna took a big bite of the gooey cheese sandwich and let the warmth travel all the way down before she let out a contented sigh. "I know if we *needed* to stay you'd make it work, but this will be fine."

A roof over their heads and a built-in babysitter. All positive things, especially if she ignored the flutter of anticipation in her belly when she thought about the fact she would be living in the same house as Brad Ford.

All that muscle and manhood, and yet he'd been gentle and cautious when he'd invited her to join him and his father. And he'd promised nothing would happen that she didn't want while they were living there—

That's where the fluttering got even stronger, because if she were to tell the honest truth, what she wanted to happen was more than nothing.

Caleb Stone came through with a vehicle for her to use. The truck was slightly smaller than the boat Tamara had her drive earlier in the day but still sturdier than her car. And as Crissy waved goodbye to her friends and Hanna headed through the snow toward Lone Pine ranch, the sense of being tossed into a strange *pick your own adventure* story rolled over her again.

"Do I get to have my own room?" Crissy asked.

"Yes, but remember we're guests in their home. We need to be polite and mind our manners. And Mr. Ford will be helping take care of you when Mommy has to go to work in the evening."

Crissy took a while to process that. "Not Mrs. Nonnie?"

"Not for right now."

Another pause. "I should make Mrs. Nonnie a Christmas card."

Resilience, thy name is Crissy. "That would be a good idea."

Crissy turned toward her, a hand on Hanna's arm as she announced excitedly, "I'm going to make Christmas cards for all the firefighters. Because they were helpers."

Hanna's throat tightened. "They were good helpers, weren't they?"

Her daughter's fingers tangled in hers for a moment until Hanna had to pull her hand free to use both hands on the wheel as they went up the long, twisting driveway. At the top of the ridge, the low bungalow that was the main house for Lone Pine ranch appeared. Weathered boards graced the outside, and mature trees surrounded it.

"Look, Mommy." Crissy pointed to the top of the roof where smoke drifted from the chimney. "Santa's chimney."

Hanna laughed, the sound surprising her. "I sure hope he's not climbing down right now, or he's going to get a hot foot."

"Santa's fireproof," Crissy informed her.

That would explain so much.

Hanna pulled into the open parking space beside two much larger trucks, taking a deep breath before coming around to help Crissy. She passed her little girl the bag Emma had loaned her then offered a hand as together they marched up to the front porch. In the windows, bright lights flickered as if they were candles.

Crissy made a soft sound of amazement as she looked out into the trees where a group of deer lifted their heads to stare back cautiously. "Are those reindeer?" she asked in an awed whisper.

From this distance, Hanna couldn't tell. "Probably whitetail."

"They're friends with Rudolph." Crissy said it with such conviction Hanna didn't have the heart to say anything else.

Then the door was swinging open, and the warmth pouring out carried with it the scent of roast beef and cinnamon.

Brad stepped aside as he welcomed them in. "Just put your things down anywhere."

Crissy slipped out of her boots and put them carefully on the mat, placing her bag neatly by the toes before coming back and catching Hanna by the hand, suddenly shy.

A deep chuckle filled the air. Hanna glanced to the opposite side of the room where a man who was much smaller than Brad stood with his hands resting on two canes. It was his father, his face familiar, but while Brad was clean shaven on both his chin and head, Patrick Ford's hair and full-length beard had gone snowy white.

His lips curled upward. "Well, look who's come for a visit."

Crissy lit up like someone had thrown the switch in Times Square.

"Mr. Patrick," she shouted, crossing the short distance of the front foyer and throwing herself at him.

Suddenly what Brad had worried would be an awkward moment turned into a bit of a free-for-all. Crissy clung to his father's knees while Hanna looked on with an indulgent smile before turning to him. "Patrick and I met a number of years ago. Obviously Crissy knows him too."

Patrick squeezed Crissy gently before turning a grin in Brad's direction. Probably proud he'd managed to pull off a fast one. He hadn't mentioned a word beyond being glad to help out needy folk during the holiday time. "I'm a volunteer reader in Crissy's class. She likes it when I use voices, just like you used to."

Crissy gaped up at Brad before a little-girl giggle escaped. "You like voices?"

His dad nodded, more serious now. "Crissy, I'm sorry to hear about your house, but in the meantime, I'm glad you've come to stay with us. I think we're going to get along just fine."

"Thank you for giving us a place to stay," Hanna offered softly.

Patrick waved a hand. "Glad to be of help. Supper will be ready in a half an hour, so we've got time to get you settled."

He gestured them away from the living room and down the long hallway. "First rooms are the office and a bathroom. Then the house splits into two directions. My room is at the end of that hallway." He pointed off to the right. "And Brad has the rooms down at the end that way."

A buzzer went off in the back, and his dad motioned for Brad to deal with it. "Put the roast on the stove," he ordered. "I'll get the girls settled."

Which was good, because it saved Brad the awkwardness of trying to figure out exactly where to put the two of them. There were four open bedrooms, but only one had access to an en suite bathroom. It made the most sense for Hanna to stay there, but...

It was the room next to his. No way on earth could he suggest she use it without the proposition coming out wrong.

Nope, it was better to let fate, spelled P A T R I C K, take control of this one.

It was strangely right to have more people at the table. Crissy asked Patrick for help in cutting up her meat, Hanna watching every move for signs of discomfort. She relaxed as time passed, and it was clear her daughter really was comfortable around both Patrick and Brad.

Brad was the one who felt incredibly awkward. Somehow they got through to the end of the meal without him tangling his tongue or dropping anything as he passed the food around the table. And afterward when Hanna insisted on washing up,

Patrick offered Crissy a broom and told her she'd have jobs to do every day as well.

Crissy spoke quietly. "Mommy says I'm good at chores."

"Good to know. I like having a helper," Patrick said. He eyed Crissy closely. "How are you at cuddling kittens?"

One little girl was about to bounce her way through the roof, quietness erased. "You have *kittens*?"

As Patrick got permission from Hanna to take Crissy to the nearby barn to visit the kittens, Brad had to smile. He'd known Patrick would thrive on this—all the time they'd been kids, his dad had been the one who nurtured their love of animals. It had been his mom who'd encouraged him to go into firefighting.

Brad tucked away the leftovers before joining Hanna at the sink. "Crissy is doing well."

Hanna moved the washcloth over the plate slowly, her chin dipping. "She talks about Mr. Patrick all the time. That's why I thought it would work for us to be here for a while. It should make it easier for her."

"Well, then, I'm glad we can help out." Only he'd been watching closely, and she was still washing the same plate she'd been on when he stepped to her side. He pulled it out of her hands and placed it in the drying rack before tugging her to face him. "And how are you doing?"

She was fighting to keep from crying, that much was clear. He just stood there and waited for a sign of what she wanted.

Hanna took a shaky breath, swallowed hard then opened her mouth to hesitantly ask, "Can I have a hug?"

Oh God. "Of course, sugar."

It was different than when she'd surprised him in the office. Then her hug had been fierce and determined, as if the motion had exploded out of her nearly the same way as his invitation to stay with them. Unlike that one, this embrace wasn't about giving, but getting.

Hanna leaned into him, and he cradled her against him. He kept his touch innocent, offering his strength. They stood there for a good five minutes, her cheek turned so her ear pressed hard against his chest, her arms wrapped around him clinging tight as if she weren't ready to stand on her own two feet yet.

She'd done enough standing on her own in the last twenty-four hours as far as he was concerned.

Slowly her breathing evened out, and when she gave him a final squeeze before stepping back slowly and wiping at her eyes, he waited a moment so she could pull herself together. Handing her a box of tissues drew a shaky laugh from her lips.

"Sorry about that."

Brad snorted, and her head shot up in surprise. "Seriously? Don't apologize for needing a hug. Not only do I understand, I'm surprised you haven't had a meltdown. And that's not any kind of judgment call on you. Being involved in a fire is traumatic."

"You can say that again," she said dryly. She stepped back farther and smiled up at him. "Okay, I promise I won't keep breaking down and crying on you. Why don't you tell me what your favourite cookies are? I can start baking tomorrow."

Crissy came running back into the room a few minutes later followed by Patrick who looked pleased as he worked his way into the room, leaning on his dual canes. "Looks as if we have a very talented cat-cuddler at our service," he informed Brad.

"There are four kittens," Crissy said as she snuggled against Hanna, looking up at her with love in her eyes. "And none of them have names yet. Mr. Patrick said I get to name them."

"That's a special treat." Hanna glanced at Patrick. "Thank you."

She was saying it for more than just the kittens, and it was clear he knew that as he dipped his chin then winked. "My favourite show starts in fifteen minutes. Anyone want to join me?"

Crissy followed after him into the living room, but Hanna hesitated in the kitchen. "Can I use your phone? I should make some calls to see what's going to happen with housing and everything else."

Brad set her up on their landline, then took off to the back rooms to call the RCMP to double check if there was anything needed for their investigation that required Hanna. He didn't want her to be surprised. Figured if he could warn her ahead of time that would probably be best.

He was stepping to his bedroom when he realized the door on the other side of his was open. And while there wasn't too much in the room, a robe lay on the bed and a pair of slippers waited on the floor beside it. Smaller slippers than he wore but far too big to be Crissy's.

He was either going to give his dad something wonderful for Christmas or a lump of coal.

Brad headed out to the barns to take care of the last couple of animals they owned. The horses bumped their noses against his hand, and Brad enjoyed the relaxing pace, but not even the familiarity of the task was enough to distract him from his current situation.

Hanna Lane was in his house. Sweet, determined, tenderhearted Hanna, who in the course of the last day had set his feet on a different path than he'd expected. Yes, he wanted to date her. And yes, his plans had always included some sort of nebulous *future and family* flavour.

But this was real. Having her and Crissy here in his house had turned *someday* into *someday soon.*

He wandered around outside, kicking up snow and staring up into the starry sky, killing time as he let his mind wander. Problem-solving the way he always had by using his feet.

There was still his brother to deal with, and more family baggage to put away, but right now the only thing he could concentrate on was her. And staying outside in the frigid cold seemed far more logical than going in and having to face her.

Sometime while he'd been in the barns, both the girls had headed off to bed, which was probably for the best. Still that meant that he was hard-pressed to simply get ready for bed, staring at the wall between their rooms and wondering...

Just wondering.

When he finally fell asleep, he was too restless to sleep well, which meant when he woke at six as usual, Brad stumbled into the kitchen to get the coffeemaker going, jerking to a stop when he realized the pot was full. And hot.

And he wasn't alone.

Brad turned slowly, blinking to wake up. Hanna stiffened where she sat at the table, her eyes sweeping over him as fiery-red bloomed in her cheeks. She got stuck staring at his waist, and that's when he realized that, like most mornings, he wore nothing but a pair of pyjama bottoms.

The fact she couldn't seem to tear her gaze off his body did something good for his ego.

But when other parts of him began to react, he stepped carefully behind the counter and offered a wave. "Sorry. Forgot."

"Coffee first, engage brain second?" She lifted her gaze to his eyes, and while she was still blushing furiously, she was smiling. She outright snickered when he picked up his empty cup and tried to take a sip. "Umm, Brad? You take anything with your cup of air?"

He glared at her without wanting to glare. Her lips simply curled up harder.

He folded his arms over his chest, lowering his voice to a growl. "Perky morning person. Damn. I rescind the invitation."

Hanna laughed. The pure bright sound broke over the kitchen and delighted him nearly as much as the fact that her eyes were once again dipping over his body in appreciation. She seemed to like his biceps.

He liked that she liked his biceps.

He pointed over his shoulder as she rose to her feet. "I'll get a shirt."

"I'll pour your coffee. Black?"

"Triple, triple," he admitted.

"Got it." She got busy at the counter, and he strode back to the hallway, but a glance over his shoulder said she was sneaking a peek at his backside as he left the room.

Brad could put up with her being a morning person.

5

Hanna stirred a third spoonful of sugar into Brad's coffee and wondered if she'd stepped into a trap.

Probably, but she wasn't truly upset about it, either. She should be. She knew too well how following her instincts could end up being life-changing and devastating, but another part of her insisted this wasn't the same thing.

When she'd been fifteen and drawn toward a certain boy, it had been enough that the attraction was there. Acting on the fledgling arousal had been a kind of rite of passage. Only in her case it had gone too far. Those fumbled attempts at intimacy had been interesting but not much more.

What that first experimentation *had* accomplished was to get her pregnant, but even that wouldn't have been a complete disaster if her partner had proven to be slightly more mature.

But he hadn't, and now here she was with an eight-year-old daughter, which made sexual attraction something she was very aware of and yet hesitant to act on.

Brad's not Jamie, her mind told her, and she knew that. But knowledge didn't make the water look any less scary to jump into. She had no idea how deep the pool would go.

Crissy was sleeping in, which was probably a good thing after a couple of mixed-up, messed-up days. Something clattered in the hallway, and she braced herself and put on a smile only to find it was Patrick entering the room.

He took one look at her and chuckled softly. "Ms. Lane. You're going to have to stop being so skittish, or you're going to hurt my feelings."

She poured a cup of coffee and held it toward him. "Not so much skittish as wanting to stay out of your way as much as possible."

Patrick settled into what was obviously his chair at the table, wrapping his fingers around the cup she gave him. "Well, that's a bunch of bull if I ever heard it. Excuse the language."

He glanced over his shoulder as if looking for Crissy.

Hanna returned to where she'd been sitting before Brad had interrupted her. "She's sleeping in. Which I don't expect to happen very often, so don't get your hopes up."

"We're usually early risers around here. Brad can be off at all times of the day and night, as well as the hours he spends at the office. Me, I'm more into puttering around." He offered her a slow nod. "I'm looking forward to you and the little missy being with us. It's a big place for an old man to ramble in by himself, and no matter how much volunteer work I do, there are a lot of empty hours in the day."

She heard noise from the hallway again. This time it was Brad, moving to the counter to pick up the cup she'd left for him. He drank deeply before shifting to the table and settling without a word.

His father snorted in amusement. "Ray of sunshine, aren't you, son?"

Brad just lifted a brow and went back to drinking.

She shouldn't have been so amused, but the level of comfort between the two men was solid, as if this teasing had started years ago and would continue for a long time into the future.

Hanna deliberately put her attention on Patrick as he gestured broadly, but she was utterly aware of the big firefighter's presence.

"Once the little miss is awake, Brad, I thought you could take the sled out and fetch a tree," Patrick said easily. "I've been putting off decorating because it's a big house and there's not much use when it's just the two of us. But since she's here, we'd better brighten the place up."

It would be easy to protest that was too much work. The sheer happiness on Patrick's face, though, and the way Brad snuck a glance at her, as if reminding her of his comment to try to make the holiday season special—

"Crissy will be over the moon if she gets to ride in a horse-drawn sled." Hanna took a deep breath and nodded her approval at Patrick. "To tell the truth, the idea makes me happy too. It's been a long time since I got to ride in a sleigh."

"You've been for a ride before?"

Brad's voice was sleep rough, and deep enough to send goosebumps racing over her skin, but she sat politely and pretended that it was just a little cold in the room. "We used to have sleigh rides at home when I was growing up." And that was enough of that memory. She forced a smile and thought of more recent times. "I think the second year we were here in Heart Falls, the community centre had sleigh rides on Boxing Day. That was around the soccer field. It was fun, but it wasn't quite the same as riding over foothills and through the trees."

Brad was watching her, his blue eyes intent as if he had questions he was holding back. She appreciated his restraint because there were certain topics she had no interest in getting into.

The past was the past.

Conversation continued, and Patrick got up and began pulling out frying pans. Crissy wandered into the room, a sleepy-eyed girl, blinking hard as she stumbled over to Hanna's side and crawled into her lap, laying her head against Hanna's chest as she slowly woke up.

"I think you found a very comfortable bed," Hanna teased.

Her daughter was tired enough to answer as if it was a real question. "Yes, only there was a scratchy pillow. I put it on the floor." Crissy lowered her voice to a whisper. "And then I used Pooh Bear as a pillow."

"That was smart," Hanna told her. "We'll go through later to make sure the scratchy pillow is fixed, but you need to be waking up so we can go get a Christmas tree."

Her words were the equivalent of feeding someone three cups of coffee. Crissy sat upright, winking rapidly to chase away the sleep still working through her system. "Christmas tree?"

"After breakfast," Hanna warned.

"That's right. We'll finish some pancakes then head out to find the perfect Christmas tree. You think you can help with that?" Patrick asked from beside the stove where he was flipping something that smelled delicious.

Crissy tilted her head. "Help with eating pancakes, or finding a Christmas tree?"

A low rumble of amusement carried from across the table as Brad woke up a little more. "Hopefully both."

It appeared Crissy was more than capable of demolishing a stack of pancakes, after which she hurried to pull on a couple of layers of borrowed clothes.

Hanna finished helping Brad load the dishwasher before moving off to see what she had to wear. Patrick greeted them at the mudroom door to cover them with extra layers of sheepskin-lined work jackets, and warm toques for their heads.

Brad came in from harnessing the horses in time to help Crissy stick her hands into an oversized pair of mitts.

Crissy laughed, holding her palms in the sky. "I look like a snowman," she said.

Brad turned to Hanna, pulling another pair of gloves off the shelf far above her head. He held them open, and she slid her hand in, very aware as his fingers brushed her wrists.

He stood from where he'd been stooped slightly, gaze firmly on hers before he broke the connection and offered Crissy a hand. "Come on. You can ride up front with me and help guide the horses."

It was too easy to follow, content to watch her daughter's delight as Brad lifted her onto the front seat of the small sleigh.

Only when he turned back to help lift her as well, she backed away, glancing to see where Patrick was. "I thought your father was coming with us."

Brad shook his head. "He'll help us unload the tree, but I was kind of surprised he even suggested it. With his legs, the deep snow is unmanageable. Still, going to cut down the tree was a tradition for him and mom."

Hanna peeked back at the house. Through the living room window Patrick was visible, resting in the easy chair, staring into space as he rocked.

"He's okay," Brad assured her. "We talked while I was harnessing the horses. He just wants a little time."

Then before she could protest, he wrapped his hands around her and lifted her onto the seat as well, his strong grip sending shivers over her.

He walked around the horses to get to the other side, the sleigh rocking with his weight as he settled. Crissy sat between them, eyes wide with delight.

"Ready to find a tree for Mr. Patrick?" Brad asked her.

Crissy nodded. "We'll find the best tree ever."

He snapped the reins. The two horses shook their heads and took a step forward, the bells on their harnesses ringing with a happy sound as they moved out of the yard and up the rolling hills behind the homestead.

~

THE MORNING WAS crisp and cold, and Brad took them as straight as possible to the section of spruce along the powerline. These were trees that had to be cut down on a regular basis anyway, and as he guided the horses along the track, Crissy quivered and shook and pointed excitedly to one tree after another.

"That one looks like it has three arms and it's reaching around to scratch its back. And look, Mommy. That one has a top hat like Frosty the Snowman."

"It does have a top hat," Hanna agreed. "But I don't think that would make a very good tree to take inside the house."

"No, we need one that's pretty for Mr. Patrick. He said he would read me some Christmas stories once the tree is set up." She turned and laid her hands on Brad's arm to tell him sadly, "All my books got burnt up, didn't they?"

It was the first time she'd spoken of the fire that he'd heard. "I'm sorry, they did. Maybe you should make a list of your favourite books, and we'll see if we can find them again."

Crissy leaned her head on Hanna, suddenly quiet.

Hanna put an arm around her and squeezed tight, a soft sigh escaping before she leaned down and pressed a kiss to her little girl's head. "I think we're getting close to finding that perfect tree. Do you think we need to sneak up on it? So it doesn't run away?"

Little-girl laughter came softer than it had before, but Crissy still smiled. "Trees don't run away."

"Neither do snowmen, but in a story anything can happen,"

Brad pointed out, glancing down to find Crissy looking up at him with wide eyes. "I think that once upon a time all the Christmas trees used to run away."

Silence fell as he made up a story right on the spot, lowering his voice and raising it during the dramatic moments until he had Crissy laughing again.

She pointed with delight at the tree he thought was probably the one they should take down this year anyway. "There it is." Excitement vibrated through her. "There's our tree, just waiting for us."

As he stopped near their target, Hanna was eyeing him with something far different than he remembered seeing before.

Oh, they'd only dated those few times, but to tell the truth, he'd been watching her for a lot longer than that. She had soft faces, and tired expressions, and gentle laughter when she was with her friends.

Right now? The way she was looking at him made his gut tighten in a whole new way. It looked as if she was fascinated. And it wasn't just lust—although as she realized he was staring back, her cheeks flushed.

She hurriedly climbed from the sled.

Crissy danced in the snow, pounding paths in circles as he got out the axe and cut down the tree. Hanna chased her daughter, laughter rising from them both.

"Mr. Brad. You have to play with the fairies," Crissy reminded him.

He tucked the axe back safely under the seat on the sleigh before raising his arms, growling as if he were a bear.

Hanna laughed as Crissy put her hands to her face and let out a scream, turning to run away as Brad chased her. He scooped her up in one arm and kept going, circling around and aiming straight at Hanna.

Her laughter faded, and her eyes widened as he caught her

up with his other arm then twirled the three of them in a circle before crashing into the nearest snow bank.

Brad made sure he landed at the bottom, working carefully to protect them. It meant Crissy landed to one side, a cloud of powder flying upward before settling on Hanna's back.

Hanna, however, had landed directly on top of him. Her slight weight barely pinned him down, but there was most definitely direct contact with the entire length of her body over his.

With her next breath Crissy demanded, "Snow angels," before popping up, moving a couple of paces away then throwing herself onto the snow again.

Hanna was still on top of Brad, her arms moving slowly so she could press her palms to his chest. She cautiously adjusted her legs, which he really appreciated, considering she had a knee directly over sensitive territory.

The arm he'd wrapped around her—he wanted to use it to squeeze her tighter. To hold her as he reversed their positions and rolled her under his body. To bring up his other hand and catch the back of her neck and tug her rosy lips within kissing distance.

What he did was let her go.

"Oops-a-daisy," Crissy sang, coming back to their rescue. "Are we going to take the tree back now?"

Brad curled up to a seated position, lifting Hanna as he moved, sliding to his feet and gingerly brushing the snow off his jeans. He moved cautiously because that quick second of contact between him and Hanna had been enough to ignite his body. "One more stop then we'll be on the way home."

Hanna wasn't looking at him, but she was smiling, and her cheeks were flushed from what he was sure was more than just cold.

He loaned the tree then lifted Crissy back into the seat, the little girl chattering away about the perfect Christmas tree resting on the sleigh behind them. He turned to give Hanna a hand up.

She scrambled past him, placing her foot on the runner and crawling onto the seat. Twirling to face him, satisfaction was written all over her expression at having gotten there ahead of him. Brad chuckled and took his place, letting Crissy help guide the horses.

He pulled to a stop outside the old settler's cabin on the top of the ridge.

"Santa's house." Crissy nodded knowingly.

It did look like something out of a postcard, with a thick layer of snow on the eaves and front porch railings. "I'm sure he uses it sometimes when he wants a break, which is why we have to take a peek to make sure it's got everything he needs."

The place didn't get used much these days except as an emergency shelter, but with a cold snap predicted over the holidays, Brad wouldn't leave anything to chance. He got down and moved toward the cabin, smiling as a hand slipped into his.

"Does Santa really live here?" Crissy asked in a little-girl whisper, the kind that ended up nearly full volume.

Brad shook his head as he reached for the door and pushed the latch open. "No. Santa lives at the North Pole. But when he's out and about, he needs safe places to stay."

"Or the elves," Crissy pointed out.

Hanna followed them in, the cold in the cabin sharp. Faint light shone through the tiny windows. "Emergency shelter?"

Brad met her eyes. "Yes. Anyone who needs it. In fact, if you wanted to stay here you'd be welcome, but it's a bit far to get to school for Crissy."

The little girl was exploring the far side of the cabin. Brad went through his checklist quickly to make sure the emergency supplies were in place and nothing had been torn apart by animals sneaking in.

Hanna looked over the place with a strange expression. Kind of happy and sad. "It's cozy."

He was about to answer when laughter spilled from the other side of the room. He and Hanna turned to face Crissy who was pointing at them. Or more specifically, pointing over their heads. Delight bubbled from her as she covered her mouth with a hand.

He and Hanna exchanged glances then tilted their heads back. Directly overhead was a batch of smooth-edged green leaves with shiny white berries, tied with a red ribbon.

"Santa left some mistletoe," Crissy said with great authority. "I saw a story about it in school. That means you have to give Mr. Brad a kiss, Mommy."

A soft sound escaped Hanna as Brad's heart began to pound.

"What kind of books are you reading?" Hanna asked under her breath.

Pretty good books, as far as he was concerned.

He fought to keep his expression neutral as Hanna turned to him. The faint light shining in the windows landed on her face and made the worry in her eyes clear.

"We don't have to," he offered softly.

To his surprise—she was always surprising him—her left brow arched up. "I'm not breaking any of the Christmas rules. If we're supposed to kiss under the mistletoe, then that's what we're going to do."

She caught him by the collar and tugged him downward sharply, planting her lips against his. Sweet and soft. The moment went on longer than he'd expected, but not nearly long enough.

He opened and closed his fingers to keep from grabbing her, wanting to catch hold of her and cling tightly so he could continue. She was pressed right up against him...

This was all he was going to get, so he was going to enjoy

every second. When she opened her lips for the briefest second and licked like a teasing kitten, he went breathless.

Hanna pulled away, cheeks flushed but grinning as if she was pleased with herself. She patted his chest then turned to her daughter with a nod. "There you go. One kiss under the mistletoe."

"My turn," Crissy demanded, rushing forward and throwing herself into Hanna's arms.

Brad stood back and watched as Hanna laughed out loud, twirling her daughter and planting kisses all over her face. A sweet, loving act made up of layers of so much connection.

He was buzzing from the brief touch. What would it be like to have all of Hanna offered to him? Complete and pure, with all her layers.

He wasn't sure, but damn if he didn't want to find out.

6

It was eight days until Christmas, and Hanna Lane was annoyed with herself.

She'd spent the rest of the sleigh ride home chatting with her daughter as if she didn't have a care in the world, but somewhere along the way she'd obviously lost her senses.

It wasn't only that she'd kissed Brad, although heaven knows that was bad enough. The fact she'd lost her mind in front of her daughter, and the potential consequences of that kind of behaviour sobered her rapidly in spite of the effervescence rioting through her bloodstream.

Kissing him had been eggnog with hundred-proof rum, the entire glass drunk far too quickly.

He stopped to drop them off at the house. "Unless you want to help me put the horses away," he offered Crissy.

Crissy looked up at Hanna, pleading in her eyes. "Please, Mommy? I'll be very good and listen carefully to everything Mr. Brad says."

"If you're sure?" Hanna said, meeting his gaze.

"Not a problem at all."

He waited while she climbed down, answering Crissy's request to drive the horses the rest of the way with patience. It was too much to take in, and Hanna retreated to the house, slipping into Patrick's domain as if she were escaping a dangerous situation. And maybe she was.

Watching Brad with her daughter wasn't the way to keep herself under control.

"You find a nice one?" Patrick leaned on the doorframe, hands heavy on his canes.

She took her worries and packaged them up, wrapping them away tightly, at least for the next while. These people had been nothing but kind, and she'd do all she could to keep her end of the bargain, which meant holiday cheer.

"It's a very pretty tree. Brad said he needs to set it in a stand to warm up and soak in water, so we can't decorate it until tomorrow."

Patrick nodded. "You can help me get out the decorations, though. They've been tucked away for a while, and I can't get at some of them with these." He tapped a hand on his legs before gesturing toward the back of the house.

One of the rooms down Patrick's side of the bedroom wing must've been his wife's. He opened the door and stood there, staring sadly for a moment before forcing a smile and tilting his head. "All sorts of doodads in here. I made this room for Connie. She's got the biggest closet any woman ever could have, and she loaded it up with frilly things. We may as well use them."

Hanna stepped in cautiously, as if she'd been given an opportunity to share something precious and beautiful.

Mrs. Ford had been handy, that much was clear. Now Hanna understood where the soft knitted blanket draped over the back of the couch had come from. The cross stitches on the walls were obviously her work as well. This room was filled to the brim with neatly organized craft supplies, including yarn and knitting needles.

Along one wall, two sturdy tables held a pair of sewing machines. A third table near the door was covered with wrapping paper. Between them was a comfortable-looking loveseat that faced the TV monitor mounted on the wall.

Patrick stepped in beside her. He sighed heavily then spoke. "She was always working on something. Even after the boys were gone. She called it her mom cave."

Hanna was still looking around when Patrick pointed at the barn-style doors covering the third wall. She pushed them aside to see row upon row of Rubbermaid totes stacked from the floor to ceiling. Each one of them was clearly labelled with brightly coloured markers on gleaming white stickers.

"Must be a half a dozen of them that say Christmas decorations," Patrick pointed out. "I shouldn't make you carry them. Brad can get them when he's back—"

"Mr. Ford, I am perfectly capable of carrying boxes of decorations."

He eyed her and smiled. "*Patrick*, I am perfectly capable, etc. etc."

She reached for the first set, pulling it forward easily on the carpet in spite of the weight. "*Patrick*. I want to help."

He nodded, then reached up and lifted the top tote—the one she was far too short to reach—and placed it on the ground beside her. "There. We'll all do what we can."

By the time Crissy and Brad were back in the house, the boxes were stacked beside the kitchen table and Patrick had pulled out his wife's recipe books to point out his favourite holiday recipes.

Not that he was demanding she cook anything, but the conversation had made its way back to cookies in a remarkably short period of time.

Brad chuckled as he put a pot of water on to boil. "I see he's got you slaving already."

Crissy climbed up in the chair next to her. "What're we going to make, Mommy?"

"Gingersnaps. And sugar cookies."

"Gingerbread men?" Crissy begged. "So we can ice them?"

"I have to agree with her," Patrick said with a slow nod, stroking his snowy white beard. "Gingerbread men taste a whole lot more delicious than simple gingersnaps."

"If you haven't already noticed, my father has a sweet tooth," Brad said in a teasing tone.

"I guess you come by it naturally, Mr. Three-spoons-of-sugar-in-my-coffee," Hanna said, without looking up from the recipe.

Laughter rolled across the room, and suddenly Hanna realized she hadn't been very polite. Truthful, but not polite.

Thankfully, Crissy hadn't noticed. Patrick continued to grin as he bookmarked a dozen pages in his wife's recipe book. Hanna fought her embarrassment and slid up to where Brad was pouring a mountain of macaroni noodles into boiling water. "I didn't mean that in a bad way," she murmured.

Brad's deep chuckle stroked her. "I'll be the first to admit I like sweet things."

She glanced up to find his gaze drifting over her. His lips were still curled into a friendly smile, but the heat in his eyes grew, and while her girlfriends might tease her that she was an innocent, Hanna knew what was going on in a man's head when he had *that look.*

Bradley Ford wasn't daydreaming about sugar cookies.

She pulled herself back, opening space between them as she straightened. "I'll wait until after lunch to start the baking. I don't want to keep you from your day, but I will need help finding everything."

"Dad will give you a hand with that, if you don't mind. I've got a few things to do first."

Sudden guilt at having consumed his entire morning rushed her. "Of course. You've already been more than generous with your time—"

"Hanna." His chuckle interrupted her, and he was no longer looking at her, instead staring into the pot as he stirred the noodles. "Promise you'll stop saying *thank you* every two minutes." He glanced over her shoulder at where Patrick was slipping through the worn cookbook, pointing at pictures and sharing stories with Crissy. "I mean it. You being here is huge. I'm the one who should be saying thank you."

He was serious and sincere, and the bit of tightness inside her relaxed slightly. "I don't want to be a burden."

"You're not, and I don't want to talk about it anymore. Grab the milk and cheese for me, please?"

She moved quickly to help, stepping back out of the way as he competently placed cutting boards and graters on the counter beside the stove. It was too easy to get enthralled as he unwrapped the block of cheese and pushed it up and down against the grater, shreds sliding into a neat pile on the cutting board. Competent and...

Hanna needed to admit it. The man was mesmerizing. The way the tendons flexed in his forearm as he adjusted his grip, the way he moved smoothly back and forth, rinsing his hands and draining the water from the noodles—

She really needed to turn away because who in their right mind got turned on while watching a man measure butter into a pot?

A low sizzling noise began, and Brad wiped his hands on the towel hanging in front of the stove. "Hey, Crissy. I need your help."

She came quickly, eyeing him with curiosity as he pulled a

stool to the counter. "I'm not allowed to turn on the stove," she told him.

"That's a good rule, especially if you're all by yourself. When you're with a grownup is the best time to learn to cook." He grabbed the wooden spoon off the counter and held it out. "Are you ready to make macaroni and cheese?"

Crissy glanced at Hanna for approval.

Hanna wasn't sure what was going on, but Brad had a point. "You follow all of Brad's instructions, yes?"

"Yes, Mommy."

"Let's get to work," Brad told her firmly, gesturing toward the pot. "Spoon at the ready, and...stir."

Hanna inched away slowly, trying to give her daughter some breathing room. It was easier after she saw how careful Brad was to make sure the situation was safe. When he started telling Crissy a story about the *secret rules of a chef*, which were cleverly disguised safety tips at a child's level, that's when she managed to turn her back and rejoin Patrick at the table.

Brad's father had been watching closely as well. As she settled, he reached over and patted her hand. "She'll be okay. That's the spiel my wife gave the boys back in the day. She taught them to cook that same way. Heck, I think that's even the stool they used to climb up on."

Hanna took a peek, but there wasn't much to see except two backs and Crissy's arm moving vigorously as she stirred. "My mom taught me how to cook as well, but..."

She stopped, suddenly unable to continue because the past was one part of her world that was impossible to think about or discuss. Coldness slipped in like always when she reminisced about her family.

No. *Not* family—simply the people who'd raised her. That was a more accurate description, considering family was supposed to mean love, and the way she'd been treated wasn't based on love.

Hanna snapped her gaze up. She'd been sitting in silence after stopping abruptly.

Patrick took a deep breath, but he didn't say anything about her sudden drop of conversation. He must have realized they'd hit a hot button because instead he pulled the cookbook forward and reopened it to the page that held the gingerbread recipe. "If you want, I can walk you through where everything is."

Hanna bounced to her feet, grateful for something to do that didn't involve feelings of rejection or sadness. She had so much to be grateful for, but as Patrick pointed at the cupboards and she slowly gathered all of the ingredients for the Christmas treat, it was impossible to completely get rid of the bitter emotions.

The goodness of being accepted and made welcome stood in powerful contrast to the memories dancing through her brain.

Brad kept his attention on Crissy until the potentially dangerous parts of preparing macaroni and cheese were done, but the entire time he was completely aware of Hanna's presence in the room.

And while she spoke with a fine, clear enunciation, all of her words were soft, fading into a gentle murmur as she conversed with his father.

There was something far too right about having her in his house, digging into the cupboards as she followed his father's attempts to remember where everything was stored. Brad was the one who did most of the cooking these days.

"Is this really going to be good?" Crissy asked with suspicion as she waited to one side for him to finish closing the door on the oven.

Brad gasped. "Have you never had homemade macaroni and cheese before?"

Crissy shook her head, staring at the cheese clinging to the wooden spoon with suspicion. She took a sniff. "It's not the same colour as what Mommy makes."

"Nope. Trust me, that's not a bad thing." He leaned in close. "Are you going to lick the spoon?"

She frowned. "Maybe?"

Laughter sounded behind them, and Brad and Crissy turned to find Hanna waiting. "Now the secret is out. I'm a boxed mac-and-cheese chef."

Crissy wrapped her arms around her mom, the spoon waving precariously. "I like your mac and cheese," she assured her.

"I like that type too," Brad informed them, "but sometimes I like to make it from scratch, the way my mom used to."

Then he pointed Crissy toward the cupboard where the plates were so she could set the table, Patrick shuffling back just far enough so the little girl could work around him.

"Is it long until lunch?" Hanna asked. "I need to borrow your phone so I can confirm my work schedule for this week."

Damn. "I'm sorry. I should've spent the morning helping get your things together instead of gallivanting across the countryside."

Hanna's eyes widened before she shook her head. "No. *No*, what we did this morning was perfect. I know we've got a lot to deal with, but it was magical to be able to go out in the snow. No matter what has to be done, it's just over a week until Christmas, and it's important to make the days special."

Relief poured over him. "Tomorrow, though. When Crissy heads off to school I can help you replace your phone and start to deal with the insurance."

She hesitated.

"What?" he demanded softly, sneaking forward and bending until their heads were on the same level.

Hanna shrugged. "You told me to stop saying thank you, but you're making it tough because you keep doing nice things."

"Of course I'm not. I mean," he continued as she raised a brow. "Yes, I suppose it is nice for me to offer to help you, but it's also logical. That's what someone does when a friend needs a helping hand."

A soft noise escaped her, and her mouth opened for a moment before she glanced away, cheeks flushing.

What was going on in that head of hers?

She turned back and nodded. "I'd appreciate your help. I'll make a list this afternoon of the most important things I can think of."

"Great idea. If you don't mind, I can help you go through the list tonight." It was too easy to show his unhappiness. "Unfortunately, I know too well all the things you need to deal with."

The timer went off on the oven, and lunch was served. Crissy pronounced the homemade mac and cheese delicious. Although she eyed Patrick with suspicion when he upended a bottle of Tabasco sauce and doused the entire surface of his plate with red.

Brad forced himself from the room and left the three of them setting up with oversized bowls and cookie sheets lining the counter. It was bittersweet to see—the last time that many utensils had been in use, his mother had still been alive. The scents of Christmas were a happy memory.

He went and found Christmas music, turning the volume up lightly in the background before taking himself off to get a bit of work done before sticky sweetness enticed him back.

Brad slipped on his coat and headed out to the barn, more to make sure he had privacy than because there was anything dire that needed to be done. He punched in a number on his phone and waited for his friend to answer.

One of the kittens from the most recent batch stalked his way along the wall joist, sliding in close and meowing piteously until Brad scooped him up for a cuddle.

Walker Stone spoke without even saying hello. "What are you up to?"

"About six foot five," Brad drawled.

"Hearty-har-har. Don't give up your day job because you're not ready for Comedy Central."

"My heart is broken," Brad offered in return. "Hey, favour to ask."

"Shoot."

"Not you, your fiancée."

There was the barest hesitation before Walker shouted Ivy's name then came back on the line. "I hear you've got house guests."

"I do. Hell of a time for a fire, but my dad's doing his best to cheer them up."

A low chuckle echoed in the background. "Of course. Your *father*. You, on the other hand, wouldn't be doing anything to try and cheer up a certain young lady. Nothing at all. Nada. It's as if she's not even there."

"Shut up," Brad muttered.

"Come on," Walker insisted. "I know how much you like her. You're sleeping under the same roof as Hanna Lane and you don't plan to take advantage of the opportunity? And I don't mean that in a creepy way."

"Nothing to take advantage of." Brad let out a heavy sigh. "I told her there were no strings attached to her staying here, and I meant it."

Walker hummed sympathetically. "Good for you. But, damn."

"Right?" But he hadn't called to get sympathy from a friend over having the woman he was interested in close and yet untouchable.

Except for that kiss...

The kiss that wouldn't have happened if there hadn't been mistletoe...

Hmmm. Maybe he needed to do some shopping.

"Hi, Brad. What's up?" Ivy Fields was on the other end of the line now.

"Just wanted to touch base. You heard about Hanna and Crissy and the fire?"

"I did. I'm glad they're okay."

"They're doing great, but it's possible shock might hit. I wanted to warn you to keep an eye on Crissy *and* her classmates —sometimes events like this can trigger bad memories. If you need anything, don't be afraid to give me a shout. In fact, why don't I come to the classroom this week to talk to the kids."

Ivy made a noise of approval. "That's a great idea. Did you want to come in the same time your father is going to be here?"

"Wednesday afternoon? Sure, that should work."

"We'll look forward to it."

Brad made one final request before hanging up, the kitten in his lap purring like a much larger-sized beast. He stroked a finger between its ears. "Time for you to go back with your siblings."

He scooped the cat up and carried it to where the current nest of kittens were piled in a warm heap. Then he made his way into the house where the sharp scent of ginger filled his nostrils and made his mouth water.

"Tell me you need a tester," he said as he walked into the kitchen.

Three heads swiveled toward him, somewhat guilty expressions on the two older faces.

Cookie crumbs decorated his father's beard, and Hanna had

a streak of icing on her cheek. The only one still grinning as she munched was Crissy.

"We're eating the broken pieces," she explained, rushing forward to escort him to his own kitchen table. "Mommy said it wasn't a good idea to decorate the gingerbread man who had no head. And Mr. Patrick said that would be like gingerbread zombies."

"Dad," Brad admonished his father. "Zombies?"

Patrick held up a bowl of icing that was tinged bright red. He didn't say anything. Just held the gory-looking mess in the air and raised a brow.

Brad laughed. "What can I help with?"

Hanna put him to work, directing him to the far side of the table where another set of icing packets waited. That sense of memory, with the past and future mixing together, struck him hard. "My mom used these every year," he told her, holding the icing plunger in the air.

She leaned in closer and spoke as if sharing a huge secret. "I don't think she taught your father how to use them."

She smelled like sugar and spice. Screw the cookies, he wanted to take a bite of her. "Nope. But I know how."

Her smile bloomed, and then she proved that in spite of being small and seemingly delicate, she had the ability to order him around as if she were a staff sergeant. For the next hour he decorated cookies, and he was only allowed to eat the ones that were broken.

Of course he had to hide his amusement when he caught Crissy carefully tearing the arm off a cookie under the edge of the table so she could pass over the pieces, her face innocent as the day.

Sweet mischief. Sweet happiness.

Across from him at the table, Patrick was smiling, the

happiest Brad had seen him in recent memory. Whatever else had brought them to this point, he couldn't feel much regret.

Hanna was back to check out his work with a strict eye. "You missed one," she informed him, pointing at a gingerbread man he'd failed to give a set of buttons.

"Easily fixed," he assured her, leaning forward to concentrate.

In the background, Patrick was wandering out of the kitchen, and Crissy, with a cookie in either hand, was following behind.

Hanna ignored them, focusing one hundred percent on him applying pressure to the icing tool—

The plastic cracked, shooting the icing in a new direction, which happened to be directly toward their faces.

He stopped immediately but it was too late. There was a set of red freckles all over Hanna's face, and from the feeling of it, his as well.

The sound started soft and low before picking up volume. Not quite a giggle and not quite a chuckle, but amusement of the purest kind. Hanna Lane was laughing as she straightened up, and she touched a finger to her skin, pulling back with red smeared across her cheek and the smallest portion clinging to her fingertip. "You have a special talent," she told him, amusement in her eyes.

"Seriously. I don't know my own strength," he offered as an excuse.

"You look funny with freckles," she teased a second before she touched her finger to his face and wiped off one of the blobs. She lifted her hand in the air and placed it in front of his face.

He was totally going to end up on Santa's naughty list, but there was no way to resist. Brad caught her by the wrist and tugged the short distance it took to suck her finger into his mouth. He swirled his tongue around the tip and licked up the sweetness clinging there.

The only protest he got was a widening of her eyes. If she'd jerked her hand back, or made a noise of distress, he would've stopped instantly.

No. What she did was take a long, slow, very shaky breath.

When she licked her lips, he was the one to call it quits. Temptation burned him hard, and the short moment of connection had sent all the blood in his body pouring south.

He pulled her finger free, keeping his lips closed around it until the last second. Staring into her eyes but seeing her nipples press to the front of her T-shirt—damn him for having really good peripheral vision.

"You do have an addiction to sweets," Hanna offered breathlessly.

Before he could answer she turned and began to tidy up, safely out of arms' reach.

7

Temptation came in six-foot-plus packages.

Hanna tidied the kitchen with Brad working quietly at her side. She'd fully expected to spend the rest of the evening hot and bothered, and desperately trying not to look as if that's how she felt.

It wasn't until she finally sat down with a piece of paper to make a list of what she needed to deal with after the fire that the heat Brad had lit inside cooled far too quickly.

Driver's license, credit card. The entire contents of her wallet. The only thing she didn't have to deal with were birth certificates and the legal work the lawyers had put together regarding Crissy and her. Those were carefully stowed in a safety deposit box.

The realization that the lawyers' office would have to replace everything they'd lost as well made her shiver. So many important papers—she was glad she'd listened to her friends when they'd recommended paying the expense for the box "just in case."

She tucked her daughter into bed that night, holding her little girl extra tight for a moment. "You okay, baby?"

"I'm not a baby," Crissy protested.

No, from the way she cuddled in tight she was a kitten same as the ones that they'd gone outside to say good night to before Crissy had her bath and crawled into borrowed pyjamas. "You're right. You're my beautiful girl. You were very good today."

Crissy made a face. "Do I have to go to school tomorrow?"

Hanna nodded. "Ms. Fields would be sad if you didn't. So would Emma and the rest of your friends."

Tears welled up in Crissy's eyes. Not fake ones, as if she was trying to get out of going to bed, but true, deep sadness. "I have to tell them all my things got burnt up."

"I know, sweetie. I'm sorry." She held Crissy, finally allowing herself to truly think about the realization that had hit while making her list.

Some things *were* irreplaceable. Not many, but things like Crissy's baby book, and the bits and pieces Hanna had saved over the years and put together as a memento—those were gone forever.

But it was her job to make sure her little girl realized that they still had what was most important. Each other. "We won't be able to replace everything at once, but after school tomorrow, we can do some shopping."

Crissy's head dipped then she kissed Hanna sweetly and cuddled in with her borrowed teddy bear and probably fell asleep before Hanna had made it back into the hallway.

She went to the living room to rejoin Patrick and Brad.

Patrick sat in his recliner near the fire. The matching chair to his sat empty in the middle of the room while Brad stretched his legs out in a much larger chair on the other side.

She hesitated.

Patrick shook his head before pointing at the empty chair.

"Connie wouldn't mind one bit if you put your feet up and relaxed."

Hanna moved quickly and sat down, the soft cushions cradling her like a warm hug. "Thank you."

"What are your plans tomorrow?" Brad asked.

"I need to work on replacing things, and I've got to find a new apartment for January first, so—"

"Hold your horses," Patrick interrupted. "Put that to the bottom of the list. The house hunting." He held up a hand to stop her protests. "Little missy, you've got enough things to worry about right now without putting something on your plate that makes no sense. It's only two weeks until the New Year. With the holidays, it's going to be impossible to find accommodation and deal with everything else. I want you to plan on staying here, and we'll make sure that you get settled somewhere good by the beginning of February."

Part of her wanted to protest, but the other part that was smarter than her sense of pride took a deep breath and accepted the help.

The memories of having to do that back when she was pregnant with Crissy rushed in again. Good memories, because good people had helped, but painful as well, because...

She met Patrick's gaze straight on. "That's a generous offer, and I know Brad told me to stop repeating myself, but thank you. I so appreciate you opening up your home to me and Crissy."

The old man nodded, a strange sort of satisfaction written in his expression. "Glad to help. That's what we're supposed to do, especially at this time of year."

She opened the notepad Brad had given her and looked down at the long list of tasks to accomplish she'd made earlier, trying to make some sense of when she'd be able to get it all done. The fire crackled and she made notes, but as the list got longer, her sense of hopelessness grew as well.

Floorboards creaked, and she glanced up to discover Brad kneeling beside her chair looking her over with a concerned expression. "You okay?"

She was *not* going to cry. "I'm a little tired."

A soft snore carried on the air. Patrick had fallen asleep in his recliner, feet outstretched and totally relaxed.

Brad chuckled softly. "So's my dad. Why don't you head to bed?" he suggested.

As tempting as it was, Hanna had dealt with this before. "If I go to bed now, working tomorrow night will be terrible. I have to stay up until at least midnight or I'll be off my routine."

His gaze drifted over her face. "You're back to work tomorrow?"

She nodded. "I have to. I'm down one job already, and I can't afford to miss any other days."

"Will you get any time off over the holidays?"

Hanna considered the calendar she'd drawn on the notepad. "Almost a week, which is good, and bad. I'll have time to get caught up on a lot of the things I need to do."

"Bad because you don't get paid if you don't work, right?" His expression softened with understanding as she nodded. "Hanna, if you need any—"

She placed her fingers over his mouth to stop him before he went too far. "Please don't offer me money. You've already done more than enough. I promise I'll ask if it gets bad."

Something flashed in his eyes. Hanna's fingers burned as the intimate connection registered, her hand over his lips. An echo of him licking her fingers in the kitchen rushed up, and suddenly she was back to running hot and cold.

He wrapped his fingers around her wrist, clearly in control as he turned her hand over and pressed a kiss to her palm.

Hanna found it difficult to take a deep breath.

He let her fingers go and cleared his throat. "On a different topic, you and I are supposed to have a date tomorrow."

It took a moment to remember, and when she did, the strange, discombobulated sensation grew in her belly. "I thought we weren't going to date while Crissy and I are living here."

"I said nothing would happen that you didn't want," he reminded her. "Dating doesn't mean we're jumping into bed. It means we're spending time together, and I don't see why we shouldn't go ahead with that part of the deal."

Could he tell how hard her heart was pounding from him mentioning sex? Hanna opened her mouth to refuse before realizing it would be an utter lie to say she didn't want to spend time with him.

The other part was the truth as well. "I'm...a little overwhelmed right now," she confessed.

He cupped her cheek, stroking his thumb gently over her skin. "Can you trust me to keep an eye on you, sugar? To not push too far, too fast?"

Maybe it made no sense, but that was the one thing she absolutely knew was true—she trusted him. "Okay."

His lips curled upward. "Okay, you trust me? Or okay to a date?"

He was going to make her say it, the meanie. "Yes, I trust you. You mentioned horseback riding, but I don't think we'll have time." She raised the notebook in the air. "I need to deal with a lot of this tomorrow. I also have to drop off and pick up Crissy from school, and I promised we could go shopping, so I need to hit the bank. And somewhere in there I have to have a nap."

"What time do you start work in the evening?"

"Usually at eight o'clock. I thought I'd get Crissy to bed before I leave, to make sure she's okay. I'll leave once she's down."

Brad grinned as a particularly loud snore rolled from the chair to their right. "We'll leave the horses for now. What if our date tomorrow involved me helping you with your list? We can take Crissy to school then get the most important things done in the morning. I'll bring you back here after lunch, and you can nap until it's time to pick her up from school."

It sounded the way everything he offered did. Far too generous. "It's not much of a date," she pointed out.

"It'll be a great date," he insisted. His gaze dropped to her lips. "I plan to hold your hand. Lots. Maybe kiss you. More than once."

There was no way he could miss the shiver that shook her from top to bottom. "Oh."

He glanced at his father before standing and offering her a hand. "Come on, sugar. If you can't go to sleep until after midnight, then we'd better find something less sleep-inducing to watch than a fire."

It felt strange and yet wonderful to slip her hands into his and let him tug her from the room. "Where are we going?"

A soft chuckle drifted her way. "Trust me."

She did, far too much, and she couldn't afford for that to be her downfall. Still, his hand was big and warm around hers as she followed at his side into a room that needed no explanation.

This time Hanna laughed. "You have a man cave."

The living room had been all about comfort, centered around the fireplace. This room had a pool table that filled half the space, while the remaining half had overstuffed chairs and a couch facing the biggest TV screen Hanna had ever seen in her life.

Brad brought her to the couch and let her settle in one corner. He took off for a brief moment before coming back with a fluffy blanket in one hand, the remote control in the other.

He sat down, not in the opposite corner, but right in the middle. His weight dented the seat cushion hard enough to cause her to roll partly toward him. Hanna's leg and hips bumped his. He flicked the blanket out and covered their lower bodies, wrapping her up in a warm cocoon between the fabric and his nearness.

It was still perfectly respectful. She'd sat this close to her friends before whenever a group of them had crowded onto the same couch.

This? Totally different.

"Christmas movies," Brad suggested. "We can do a countdown of the top ten all-time best holiday classics."

"What if my top ten are different than your top ten?" Hanna teased, surprised she managed to get the words out.

"Well, that would be a travesty because *my* top ten are the *ultimate* top ten."

He clicked on the power, turned to Netflix and started up a movie. And before she could say anything, he reached over and caught her fingers in his. Holding her hand on top of the blanket as the action unfolded on the screen before them.

Once her heart rate slowed slightly, she found herself relaxing against him, eventually leaning her head on his shoulder. Letting his presence give her a small moment of pleasure.

Tomorrow was back to the real world and everything she had to do to take care of herself and her daughter, but right here and now, she was going to enjoy the pocket of peacefulness.

BRAD COULDN'T REMEMBER the last time he'd had an evening end with his date's head on his shoulder, the woman sound asleep.

Hanna had held on until about eleven forty-five, at which point he didn't think it was worth wiggling to keep her awake the way he'd done all the previous times she'd started to nod off.

The fact she was comfortable enough to sleep cuddled against him was a good thing. Or at least, he tried to reassure himself that it wasn't because he was the most boring person on the face of the earth.

He'd have to assume his promise to go slow and be trustworthy had been accepted at face value. Which is why he had the ability to spend that last fifteen minutes staring as she breathed evenly, chest rising and falling against his arm. He'd kept hold of her hand until she wiggled it free, curling her fingers under his biceps and burrowing in tight, which was equally acceptable in his book.

Her lashes lay against her cheeks, and he was struck by how privileged he was to have her in his home. Utterly aware of how hard the next days would be for her, and wishing all over that he could take away the burden.

He could have sat there staring for hours. Instead, he woke her gently, sliding from under the blanket and easing away as she made it to her feet and blinked hard.

Two minutes later she was safely behind her door, soft movements of her getting ready for bed enough to make him turn on his heel and head back to the living room to see if his father was still there.

Patrick was awake, leaning forward and staring into the fire. His head dipped rhythmically, as if listening to a conversation only he could hear.

Brad leaned on the doorframe. "I'm headed for bed," he announced.

His father glanced over his shoulder, blinking in surprise. "I should do the same. Although I suppose I'm just changing locations—I can sleep here as easily as I can there."

Brad stepped forward and offered a hand to assist his father to rise to his feet. "You'll sleep sounder in your bed."

"I'll only sleep for as long as my brain will let me," Patrick complained. "Keep thinking about your brother. Wish there wasn't this wall between us."

Patrick leaned heavily on his canes to move forward. He looked older than usual, not because of his motion but because of the weariness in his face.

The way he always looked when he talked about Mark.

Brad kept his mouth shut until he helped his dad into his room. "Give it time. Keep the door open."

His father nodded, then offered a wave goodnight, leaving Brad with his thoughts and frustrations.

Mark wasn't a rotten person. He just had priorities wrong, as far as Brad could tell. Money meant everything to his brother, in the "it flows through his fingers faster than he can make it" kind of way.

He took himself off to bed, carefully opening the door leading into the shared bathroom, but the door on her side of the room was closed. Hanna was long gone to sleep.

He tried his best to be up and moderately happy in the morning, but that was asking a little much. Patrick drifted through the room, answering Crissy's questions about the next time he'd be in their classroom.

"Ms. Fields said we can read Christmas stories when you're there because it's the last day before the holidays," Crissy told him excitedly before her face turned sad. "It was on an announcement paper in my backpack that got burnt up."

"I'm sorry about your backpack, but thank you for reminding me," Patrick said, pointing to a paper bag on the counter. "It's not new, but I found something this morning for you to use."

Crissy left her bowl of cereal and scurried across the room, bringing the bag with her to Hanna and crawling into her mom's lap to open it.

As the straps of the brightly flowered bag came into view, Crissy made a low sound of happiness. "It's so pretty."

Brad turned his attention on his father. Patrick wore something near a smile but not quite, fading in and out. "It was my wife's. She used it when she went to town for special events. It's got strings to close it up tight and a hidden zipper compartment. There's even a strap to wear across your body. Better than a backpack."

Crissy squirmed out of Hanna's lap and raced to Patrick's side to let him show her all the secrets.

A soft touch settled on his shoulder. Brad glanced up to see Hanna waiting there, fighting for composure.

He trapped her fingers, giving them a squeeze.

Then a dancing little girl was in front of him, flowered strap crossing from shoulder to hip as she twirled to show off her gift. "This was your Mommy's," she informed him before planting her hands on his knees and leaning forward to tell him earnestly, "I'll take good care of it, I promise."

"My mom would be pleased to see her bag going to school." He glanced at his father. "Seriously. Mom liked to make people happy."

Patrick nodded. "That she did."

The morning chaos slipped into a familiar routine as breakfast was finished and teeth were brushed. Brad ended up with three people in his truck, Crissy in a booster seat he'd grabbed from the emergency supplies at the fire hall the previous day.

He waited by the school as Hanna dropped Crissy off, walking her to the door and giving her a kiss. The flash of the brightly coloured bag was the last thing visible as Crissy slipped away.

Hanna climbed into the truck and stared out the front window, obviously lost in thought, which he understood, yet at the same time he wanted to be there for her. He reached over, pulled off her left glove and slipped her hand into his, wordlessly aiming them for the bank.

Her gaze dropped from the window to their hands. She

glanced up at him then back at their hands, but didn't say anything.

By the time she got back in the truck after the third stop, though, Brad grinned when she was the one who reached over and tangled their fingers together on top of the booster seat.

By eleven thirty they'd finished all of the tasks they could do in town, including a visit to her insurance company. He'd walked in with her on that one, standing back, but there if she needed help—he *was* the Fire Chief. If he could make anything go faster, he was going to.

Finally, Hanna stepped out onto the boardwalk, taking a deep breath before letting it out slowly. Brad tucked himself next to her to protect her from the wind that was swirling snow around them.

"Are you done?"

She leaned on the wall behind her and lifted her eyes to his. "For now? I am beyond done."

"Lunchtime." He didn't wait for an answer. He was starving, so she had to be as well. "Come on."

She walked hand-in-hand with him into Buns and Roses before her fingers slipped away.

He glanced down to see her cheeks were rosy red, far brighter than they'd been outside in the cold wind. Ahead of them Tansy Fields was eyeing them with a great deal of curiosity.

She popped out from behind the counter and came over to wrap Hanna in a tight hug. "I'm sorry, honey. I heard about the fire. I'm glad you and Crissy are okay."

Hanna nodded. "Thanks. Brad's helping me get things straightened out with the insurance and everything."

It sounded an awful lot as if she was giving an explanation for why they were together, which was all right, except she didn't say a thing about the fact that this was a date, indicating Hanna was still attempting to deny it.

As Tansy headed back behind the counter, Brad slid closer to Hanna, slipping his arm around her waist and turning her toward the menu as if it was the first time either of them had seen it. "Have something to warm you up, sugar. It's been a long morning."

The expression on Tansy's face was totally worth it, and suddenly something nipped him, hard, on the waist. He jerked upright before realizing Hanna had slipped her hand under his jacket and pinched him.

He peeked down, trying not to grin.

She leaned in close. "Behave," she warned.

"This is me behaving," he murmured back.

Thank God she laughed, the soft sound rolling over him and making his heart pound. And when she didn't run away, but curled against him as they put in their orders, something inside him melted.

He liked how brave she was. He liked how she'd been so resilient all morning, facing questions and uncertain timeframes.

They tucked themselves behind a table in the corner. Christmas music played cheerfully in the background, Hanna's cheeks bright red as she pulled off her toque and scarf and tucked them into the pocket of her borrowed coat. "Thank you for lunch."

"You're welcome." He eased his chair around the corner so they were closer to each other rather than directly across, placing his hand casually on the tabletop, palm up.

When she didn't check to see who might be watching before lowering her fingers to his, that warm spot inside got even gooier.

She lifted her gaze to meet his, blinking shyly. "This is a funny date."

"I think it's a great date," he assured her, stroking his thumb over her knuckles, breathing in deep and letting his happiness show.

She stared at his fingers, her tongue sneaking over her lips. Everything in him tightened.

He forced himself to keep his touch gentle. "It was a productive morning, as well. Sounds as if you've got all the right balls rolling, and now you're stuck on the waiting part."

Hanna wrinkled her nose. "The part I hate the most. And it's the government, so getting documents, especially over the holiday season, is going to be nearly impossible."

"Another reason for you not to worry about moving out until February," he reminded her. "It will take as long as it takes—there's no use panicking over the rest of it."

She opened her mouth, and he was certain she was going to say another *thank you* when she dipped her head firmly and changed the topic. "All the offices I clean are closed Boxing Day and the rest of the week, so that will be a good chance to get caught up on anything I need to, or if I have to go to Calgary for any documentation."

He thought of something else. "I know you made a bunch of calls last night, but is there any family you should get in touch with? To let them know about the fire so they're not worried when they try to call on Christmas Day?"

Her fingers went absolutely still, and before he could catch her, she'd slipped them away, clutching her hands together in her lap as she stared down. Shaking her head.

So different from the warm and giving woman he'd spent the morning with. This Hanna looked like a puppy someone had kicked.

"Hanna? What's wrong?" he asked softly, lowering his voice.

She took a deep breath. "I have no family except Crissy."

He waited, leaning away as Tansy brought their food to the table. Desperately hoping this wasn't the moment Hanna's friend would choose to tease.

Miracle of Christmas miracles, Tansy either was too busy to

stay or she'd caught the gist of the moment, because she gave a quick finger wave and hurried away.

Hanna picked up her spoon and stirred the soup, thick chunks of vegetables rolling to the surface as savoury-scented steam curled upward.

"*Hanna.*" Her name came out as if he were begging, and he was in a way. He wanted that bright, happy woman back. The one who'd been there only a moment earlier. "I'm sorry I asked a question that touched a nerve."

She put down the spoon, determination on her face as she reached across the table and curled her fingers over his fist, squeezing in reassurance. "You didn't do anything wrong. I'm just surprised you didn't know this gossip. I haven't seen or heard from my parents in years, and I'm an only child."

Another family with internal tension. Unfortunately, it was all too common. "I'm sorry. My brother doesn't come around very often, and when he does, there's inevitably a fight."

"With you?" she asked.

"With Dad, to tell the truth."

Her eyes widened. "How on earth could someone fight with Patrick? He's the most agreeable, kindest man I've ever met. With a heart of gold."

He gave her back her hand and pointed at her spoon to get her to start eating before the food got cold. "I'm glad you think my father's amazing. I'm actually kind of jealous."

She stopped with the scoop of thick broth halfway up, her mouth hanging open. "Jealous?"

"It's good you like him," Brad told her, smiling wickedly. "But you're *my* girlfriend."

Her spoon dropped with a clatter, and she grabbed her napkin to wipe up the splatters. "*Brad.*"

He offered his napkin as well. "Did you just call me a brat?"

"If the boot fits," she offered.

Food took precedence, easy conversation and ready smiles returning. Brad tucked away the bit of information about her family for future conversation, and that was the end of it until they got home.

His dad had left a note on the table by the front door. He'd gone shopping but would be home in time for supper.

Hanna headed down the hallway to take her nap when she stopped, turning to examine Brad intently. "We haven't really gone on enough dates for you to call me your girlfriend."

"Does it really have anything to do with how long we've been seeing each other?" he insisted, stepping closer. "Hanna, I didn't ask you out because I thought we'd have fun and fool around for a couple of months then go our separate ways. I *like* you. A lot. I don't know where this is going to end up, but I want you to be thinking about me—about us—seriously."

He was only inches away now, her head tilted back so she could look up at him.

Hanna swallowed hard.

He pointed above their heads to where he'd fastened a bunch of mistletoe on the far side of the rafter where it wasn't noticeable until he stood right in that spot.

"You *are* a brat," Hanna said softly.

"We don't want to break any Christmas rules," he reminded her before tucking his fingers under her chin. He inched forward, slow enough she could escape if she wanted, as he brought their lips together.

A soft touch. Once. Twice, before deepening the kiss. Demanding a little more, and when Hanna willingly opened her lips so he could sweep in, everything in him tightened to rock.

Except his blood which seemed infused with effervescence, or maybe helium, because his feet were about to float off the ground.

Her hands landed on his shoulders, fingers digging as she

held him, neither pushing away or pulling him closer. Right where he was seemed fine by him.

The kiss went on and on until his head was ready to explode. He was one step away from—

No, he was *taking* a step away, smile firmly in place as he backed up.

Hanna blinked at him, breathing shakily.

"Sweet dreams," he told her. "I'll wake you when it's time to pick up Crissy."

He turned his back and walked away, whistling happily.

8

Sweet dreams? Oh, she was having dreams, all right. But sweet wasn't the word, because if there had been any real sugar involved, it would've caramelized in the first thirty seconds.

Her body had still been tingling as she crawled between the sheets. Hanna had refused to go over every second of the date, or let her mind linger on the hand holding, or how good it felt to have him with her all morning.

Although it had turned out to be impossible to push the kiss from her mind. In fact, that's what she had to have been thinking about as she fell asleep because...

Dreams. *Hot* ones. Ones where all of her clothes magically disappeared, and she was no longer in her bed but in Brad's, and from there things got a little hazier in detail, but the heat remained—flaming hot, achingly hot.

Maybe there was something good about the heat, though, because eventually as her limbs relaxed, she fell into a deep sleep. The sensation of big, careful arms holding her felt far too comforting.

When she woke, Hanna rolled and eyed the clock. She had fifteen minutes before she needed to crawl out of bed, so she stretched lazily, feeling a *snap crackle pop* along her spine.

It was nice to not have to rush. It was nice to feel as if she'd accomplished some good things that morning, even though, as Brad had pointed out, now she was at the hurry-up-and-wait stage.

She slipped into the washroom, brushing her hair and examining the dark circles under her eyes. She was a vision of beauty these days.

The door on Brad's side of the bathroom opened and she twirled, hands rising to cover her body. "Stop. I'm in here—"

Only it wasn't Brad. Instead, a man with blond hair stood in the doorway. His eyes dropped over her but Hanna didn't see anymore. She screamed and swung her brush at his head. The instant the heavy-backed object made contact she let go, racing out the opposite door and through her bedroom.

Two steps into the main hallway she slammed into another body, swinging her fists and fighting until she recognized Brad's voice.

"Hanna, *stop*. What's wrong?"

She went limp in his arms, clutching his waist. "There's a man in my room. Our room. The *bathroom*," she finally got out, clinging tightly to his torso but squirming behind him like a child in hiding.

Brad straightened to his full height. He pushed her door open just as the man came out of Brad's room.

Hanna clutched at Brad's hips. "That's him."

"Mark?" Fury threw the name from Brad's lips. "What the hell are you doing in my room?"

"Checking out the decorations. Figures. As soon as you knew the place was yours, you started hauling in women."

"You're disgusting," Brad said. He stepped forward, keeping

his body between Hanna and the other man, forcing an opening for Hanna to be able to reach her bedroom door. "Hanna, go get dressed."

She vanished into her bedroom, closing the door and locking it behind her. She raced across the room to the bathroom and did the same to that lock, and only then did she take a breath.

Out in the hallway, shouting continued. Not on Brad's part—his comments were now few, deep and controlled. It was the other man who'd raised his voice, making comments about favouritism and floozies.

That was a new one. She'd never been called a floozy before. She'd heard slut and whore, which, compared to floozy, were whole lot nastier.

A crash rang out as a body slammed into one of the walls. Mark, from the sound of the curses that followed.

Hanna's hands shook as she pulled on her clothes, moving determinedly because there was no getting around it. She had to go into the main part of the house to get her keys so she could grab her daughter.

Things had gone suddenly quiet. She stole down the hallway on tiptoes, peeking around corners before committing to step into the front foyer.

Brad waited for her at the front entrance. He checked her over carefully, even as he shook his head. "I'm sorry."

"Who was that?"

"My brother."

"The one who likes to fight with Patrick?"

Brad nodded. "I took his key away. There's no way he can get back in the house unless he breaks something, and I told him if he did that I'll not only call the police, I'll call an ambulance."

The implication was easy to understand. Mark would *need* the ambulance—

The knot inside Hanna loosened, although she didn't like to

think about why the violence was so reassuring. Obviously, she was far more bloodthirsty than she'd imagined.

Brad's arms went around her, and she stepped against him, shaking as she took a deep breath then relaxed. "He surprised me, that's all. He didn't do anything."

"That's the only reason he's still breathing," Brad said softly. "Hurting, but breathing."

She glanced down, lifting his hand to check his knuckles. Sure enough his right hand was all roughed up compared to when she'd held it at lunch earlier that day. "I hit him too," she confessed. "With my hairbrush."

A soft chuckle escaped Brad. It sounded wrong, and yet right. As if he was proud of her. "That explains why Mark's nose was dented before I started."

The alarm sounded on her watch—the one she'd set to warn her so she'd never be late to meet Crissy. "I have to go."

He rubbed her back once more then released her. He cursed softly and reached for his coat, jamming his feet into his boots. "I'll drive."

She shook her head. "We're going shopping."

"So? I still need to do some Christmas shopping." He pulled a toque on his head then motioned her out the door. "Seriously. Hanna, you can't drive yet. You're shaking, and I want to make sure the bastard took my warning to heart and left the mountain."

She wasn't about to argue. Her entire body was quivering, and she didn't have time to settle down, considering school was nearly out.

By the time they picked up Crissy and did some shopping, it was four-thirty. They got back to the house to be greeted by the scent of frying hamburger meat and more Christmas music playing.

Tacos for supper were followed by decorating of the tree, and the day ended with another trip to the barn to visit the kittens.

Crissy turned quiet as she cuddled them, her enthusiasm from earlier muted.

Hanna stroked a finger over the soft fur-baby in her daughter's lap. "Are you okay, sweetie?"

Crissy nodded slowly before shaking her head. "I wrote a letter to Santa. We were supposed to mail them today, and I didn't have mine."

Her sadness was tangible. Hanna curled her arms around Crissy and hugged her tight, pressing their cheeks together. "There's still time," Hanna assured her. "You know Santa uses magic mail service."

"I know. Mrs. Fields helped me write another one already, but it was a really *good* letter," Hanna complained.

This time it was easier to smile, patting her daughter on the back. "I bet your new one was just as good. Are you ready for bed now?"

"Almost." Crissy went through all the motions of getting ready but when she was in bed and staring up at Hanna, her lower lip quivered. "You *have* to go to work?"

Hanna sat on the edge of the bed. "Oh, sweetie. Yes. Mr. Patrick is here to keep an eye on you. You don't need to be scared."

"I'm not scared," Crissy insisted. "You're the one who almost got burnt up. Santa took care of me." She lowered her voice. "He told me to hide. What if he doesn't tell you to hide?"

The bands wrapped around her chest tightened, and Hanna squeezed her little girl, not quite sure what Crissy was talking about, other than being afraid. "I am glad Santa was taking care of you, but Mommy is going to be okay."

"Promise?"

Hanna sat back as she drew an X over her heart. "Promise."

Crissy wiggled up on her knees and threw her arms around

Hanna's neck, kissing her hard before plopping down on the mattress. "I'll see you in the morning," she said softly.

"Mommy will kiss you when I get home." She kissed her before she left, as well, heading into the hallway.

"I'll take care of her," Patrick promised. "Don't you worry."

The next moments turned out to be some of the hardest Hanna had ever faced. Leaving that warm, safe haven and going out to the truck where her cleaning supplies waited. Driving away, the homey lights of Lone Pine fading behind her as she headed down the road.

Facing the fears that she hadn't even realized were there. Like leaving her little girl and going back into the darkness—

Hanna gripped the steering wheel tighter and kept going, because that's what she always did. She kept struggling forward, no matter how hard.

BRAD FINISHED CLEANING THE KITCHEN, chuckling as he put away the fifth pot. This was why his mom had always been reluctant to let his dad cook. The man couldn't fry an egg without using three pans.

The house had gone quieter after Hanna had left. The settling creaks and sighing noises from a warm house on a cold day mixed with the Christmas carols still drifting from the living room. His dad had pulled out a stack of ancient records earlier in the evening and absolutely fascinated Crissy by showing her how the magic Frisbees produced noise.

Now his father's canes echoed like slow drumbeats on the wooden floor as he made his way into the kitchen.

"Put on the kettle," Patrick ordered.

Brad moved to obey the request, sliding a few Christmas

cookies out of the full cookie jar onto a plate and plopping them in front of his father. "How are you feeling?"

He'd caught his father rubbing his legs earlier in the evening, a sure sign that the weather was getting ready to change.

Patrick made a face. "Oh, they ache, but they still get me where I need to go, so I don't have much to complain about. I want to talk to you about something."

Brad finished wiping his hands on the towel, hanging it to dry before joining his father at the table. The wind howled, shaking the windowpanes, the yard light flickering as snow whirled in front of it.

"Storm moving in?" Patrick asked.

There was another thing that made Brad smile. "You didn't watch the news tonight. I think that's the first time in years you haven't been glued to the screen all evening."

His father grabbed one of the cookies and began turning it in his fingers, fidgeting. Definitely fidgeting. "Well, yeah, I was busy."

Busy playing with an eight-year-old who looked at him with wide eyes and delight as he'd showed her how to carefully balance a quarter on the record player needle to keep it in firm contact with the vinyl to produce the beautiful music.

Brad chose not to tease. Instead, he helped himself to a cookie, pausing to admire what had to be one of Crissy's decorating attempts.

"When were you going to tell me that Mark showed up?" his father asked sternly.

A streak of anger rushed through Brad, but he chose to bite off the head of his gingerbread cookie instead of responding too soon. By the time he'd finished destroying the sweet treat, he was able to speak with control. "He showed up. I told him he wasn't welcome unless invited. That's about all there is to it."

His father stared at him, fingers tapping on the table. "Hanna seems a lot more perky than I expected, considering."

"I expect shock from the fire is still going to hit," Brad told him quietly. "Crissy too. So be ready for it if it happens while you're here with her alone."

Patrick hummed thoughtfully. "I want you to give me some hints of what to do if that happens, but *that's* not what I was talking about."

Brad paused. "I don't know what you mean, then."

He got the look from his father that was usually reserved for those moments when he was being extraordinarily dull and clueless. "A total stranger barged in on her. You don't think that might have scared her a little? Although I know Mark would never do anything to hurt her, she didn't know that."

"She was scared, but she still defended herself." Brad fought for second before giving in and letting his grin show. "She didn't quite break his nose, but she made a good attempt."

Patrick shook his head. "I hope he grows up someday. I don't know why he's got to be like this."

Brad got up to answer the whistling kettle, but he spoke firmly to his father. "It's not your fault—his behaviour. I don't know what Mark was doing here, but Hanna seemed to recover nicely."

His dad waited until they were both seated at the table again before proceeding to poke into Brad's calm and orderly world.

"I met Hanna for the first time shortly after she came to town," he shared. "She was at the police station getting a security check done so she could do her cleaning and whatnot. I was getting mine so I could volunteer with the kiddies."

The security that schools and other places used for volunteers was something Brad thoroughly approved. After his mom died, being a volunteer had become the number one distraction in his father's life.

"You've known her for a lot longer than I have," he pointed out.

Patrick's gaze caught him, clear and sharp. "You're not going to let her get away, are you?"

Blunt. "None of your business," he said, mainly because he knew it would make his father grin.

Only Patrick didn't smile. "That girl has got some bad memories from when she was growing up. I know we're going through a rough spell with your brother, and all, but between me and Connie, you boys had a good upbringing. You *knew* we were there for you, and that you were loved."

Brad thought back to the few cryptic moments when Hanna had spoken about growing up. She'd never mentioned her family without stopping in midstream. "You saying Hanna didn't have that?"

"I'm saying you really should talk to the woman. Make sure she knows you're not just looking for a good time."

Resisting the temptation to roll his eyes was far more difficult than he'd expected. "I didn't know you were taking up a new hobby," he mumbled at his father.

Patrick raised a brow.

"Seriously, if you want to be a matchmaker, there're a couple of your friends who I think are well beyond the age they should make a move."

His father laughed out loud. "Yeah, well, it's tough to teach old dogs new tricks. But you need to walk careful but still make it clear what's going on in that head of yours. Don't keep secrets."

"I'm trying not to scare the woman," Brad pointed out. "Straight-up announcing what I've got planned probably lands under the category of *ways to freak her the hell out*."

He didn't think he had to mention that he had basically done that very thing only hours earlier.

"Not necessarily," Patrick assured him. "But probably the

best way for you to find out what she really needs is to talk to her."

Which sounded like an amazing idea. Brad drained his cup and got to his feet. "You got things under control here?"

Patrick glanced at his watch. "You're going out? Now?"

"If you're good with it, yes." He placed his hands on the table and leaned forward, allowing his grin to break free. "Someone gave me the very good advice that I should talk with my girl. Fortunately, I know exactly where to find her."

As he turned and left the room, his father's chuckle danced on the air with the music.

Brad snuck down the hall and opened the door to Crissy's room carefully, peeking in on her. She was curled up in the middle of the bed with a pile of pillows around her, nestled like a kitten. Her breathing was soft and even, and Brad didn't try to fight the strange new sensation curling through him as he watched her sleep.

He closed the door quietly and pulled on a thick coat before heading into the cold. The entire drive down the hill into town he mulled over the fact that, while he'd come back to Heart Falls with the intention of making it his home, he'd never expected to find someone like Hanna, with someone like Crissy, who were both so perfect for him.

He didn't think most guys daydreamed about becoming a dad the way women seemed to obsess about having a baby, but he wanted a family. Seeing Crissy smile, seeing her sadness wiped away as Hanna spoke softly to her—being a part of the little girl's life appealed to him as much as the other parts of finding a partner.

Oh, he wanted Hanna. There was no doubt about how much he was looking forward to moving ahead with their physical relationship.

But he wanted just as much to have Crissy in his life. To have her ask to be read books and to listen as she shared stories about what she did at school. Maybe that made him strange in the eyes of the world, but so be it.

He didn't really give a damn what the world thought.

He pulled in behind Hanna's borrowed truck and made his way to where she was visible vacuuming inside the local dentist's office. He rapped on the glass door, and she jerked upright, confused until she spotted him.

She smiled for a split second before her eyes widened and she rushed forward, worry overtaking her expression.

The instant she jerked the door open he offered calmly, "Crissy is fine."

She stepped back, hand on her chest, relief streaking across her face as he snuck inside, closing and locking the door behind him. "You scared me."

"Sorry about that, but I didn't know if you'd hear if I phoned, and I didn't think a call would scare you any less. I checked her right before I came. She was sound asleep."

Hanna tilted her head and examined him. "Why are you here?"

He offered her his widest grin. "To help."

One brow arched higher than the other. "Because cleaning is something they teach in firefighting school?"

He brushed his fingers over her cheek. "Actually, yes. Not the cleaning part, but the bit about how it might be hard for you to be alone, back in a situation similar to when you recently experienced a traumatic event."

She stood motionless for a turn before pressing her cheek against his hand, as if to assure him she wasn't trying to run away. "Oh."

He stepped closer, keeping hold of her as he leaned in and stole a kiss.

He backed up reluctantly, happy at the way her pulse

pounded visibly at the base of her throat. "How's the cleaning going?"

Hanna swallowed hard. She regrouped before answering with forced perkiness in her voice. "Great. It's going great. I need to finish vacuuming then I can mop, and this office is done."

"Great to hear. What can I help with?"

9

There was no use in arguing with the man—that much was clear from the determined set of his shoulders. For whatever reason, she had a helper tonight.

Hanna shrugged and pointed at the garbage bags she'd stacked by the entrance. "If you haul those to the dumpster, I don't have to do it later."

"Got it, boss." Brad offered a salute before heading off to work.

Hanna focused on her tasks, but there was an extra bit of warmth surrounding her as she pushed the vacuum behind rolling chairs and into the corners.

It had been nerve-racking to come downtown on her own. Having Brad show up was a special kind of goodness she hadn't expected. It made a difference.

He waited on the sidewalk when she pulled the door closed behind her and locked it, an icy cold wind sweeping around them as she tucked the keys away in her pocket. "Thank you for coming out."

"No problem. Where're we off to next?" he asked.

"Brad. You can't help me all evening," she protested.

"Yes, I can."

Oh brother. "I don't have the energy to fight with you," she informed him before whirling on her heel and marching to her borrowed truck.

Sure enough, he followed her across town to a small nondenominational church that was last on tonight's list. The outside was all lit up with a nativity scene, and she stopped instinctively, gaze drawn to the carving of Mary, baby belly and all, who stood beside the manger. Joseph's arm was wrapped around her shoulders.

The church was on the loop where Hanna had walked Crissy home on school days, and the logistics of switching out a pregnant Mary and slipping baby Jesus into the manger on Christmas morning had fascinated her daughter.

Today Hanna's thoughts wandered more to the time when she'd been that pregnant woman, baby belly sticking out so far her balance had been off. She hadn't had anyone to put a hand around her shoulders, and the whole no-room-at-the-inn thing—

Been there, done that.

She tore her gaze away and determinedly stomped up the stairs as if she could walk away from the memories.

She'd almost forgotten Brad was on her heels until she came to a sudden stop inside the doors. He caught her arms instead of slamming into her and knocking her to the ground.

"Oops."

Hanna rotated guiltily. "Not your fault. I wasn't paying attention."

His gaze sharpened as he examined her face, tugging off her gloves and pulling her with him farther into the sanctuary. "What's wrong?"

She shook her head, about to insist it was nothing when her compulsion to speak truthfully got hit with a double whammy. If she was going to lie, it wasn't going to be while standing in the middle of a church.

She tucked her fingers into his and tugged him sideways, bringing him to the side of the sanctuary where a long bench was placed against the back wall. In the church where she'd grown up, that's where the families with young children had sat so they could get out quickly if a child got too noisy.

She wasn't even sure why she wanted to tell him anything, other than they were in church. Maybe that was enough to pull a confession from a person. "I was thinking back to when I was pregnant with Crissy."

Brad wrapped his fingers around hers, warmth flooding her as he rubbed gently. "I've always assumed that wasn't a particularly positive time, but I know you love her. Does that make for both happy and sad memories?"

Hanna nodded. "She wasn't planned, obviously. And the boy I'd been with wasn't about to let an accident screw up his life. He told me he'd pay for an abortion, but if I wanted to do anything else, I was on my own."

Brad cursed softly, but he kept his grip on her fingers controlled. "I'm glad you chose to have her. She's a beautiful child, Hanna."

"She's my heart," Hanna shared softly. "But those days were hard." Which was an understatement of extraordinary measures.

"Where's your family?"

The words came out softly, but they still cut. It was the question she wasn't ready for and yet the real reason why her feet suddenly felt like lead. "Southern Alberta. It was just me and my parents. When I told them I was pregnant..."

She stalled for long enough that Brad made a noise, deep and rumbling in his chest, and the next thing she knew, Hanna was sitting in his lap.

She squirmed, but his arms were locked tight around her. "Brad, we're in a church."

"And you need a hug. Those two things aren't mutually exclusive." He squeezed her tight for a moment, his chin resting on top of her head, and it was easier in a way because he couldn't see her face. He was completely attentive, his body language told her that, but not having to look at him made it easier to continue.

"My pregnancy didn't go over well." She still wasn't quite sure why she was telling Brad this, but the ball of hurt she kept inside, holding in her past—one small corner of the string began to fray and unravel as her words slipped free. "*He* called me a few names, then *she* told me to get out. They refused to have me under their roof even one more night."

If anything, his arms tightened, and his lips moved against her temples. "They were wrong. They don't deserve to have you in their life."

"I know. I really do know."

She sat motionless, wondering exactly how brave she could be. Yet—this was Brad. The man who had insisted he was her boyfriend. They'd been dating for such a short time, only she knew one solid truth.

She trusted him more than she'd trusted anyone in years.

She tilted her head back and looked into his bright blue eyes, reaching to run her palm over his cheek then lifting higher so her fingers stroked the scratchy surface of his head. Touching him and centering herself in the process.

"You said it's common to have shock hit after something like the fire. Does that include strange behaviour, like wanting to tell someone something very serious?"

His gaze drifted to her lips. "I don't know if that's shock, or just a sign that two people are learning about each other."

Hanna screwed up her courage and went for it. "I know you're serious, about the girlfriend thing, and the idea makes something inside me quiver. I think I want you to be my boyfriend, but I'm so scared. I can't quite wrap my brain around someone as good and brave and kind as you wanting someone like me, when everyone who was supposed to love me, rejected me."

His expression right then—it looked as if he were ready to take on the world for her. He caught her wrist and pressed her palm to his mouth so he could plant a kiss in the center before pulling back and speaking with crisp authority.

"Sugar, their lack of love was never about you. Anyone who had an issue, it's totally their problem. They hurt you like hell, but that's on them." He leaned his forehead to hers and stared into her eyes. "Thank you for being honest. We're not making any decisions right now, but I'm glad to hear you don't think I'm a terrible idea. I can be patient, but I'm not going to give up."

Another bit of the cord around her heart unraveled. The pressure inside turning softer, more hopeful. "Please don't give up."

She let him hold her and took total of advantage that his closeness let her twine her arms around his neck so she could soak in his warm masculine strength.

They sat there for another five minutes before she sighed. "I need to get to work. And considering the time of year, I want to do an extra good job here."

"Tell me what to—" A soft yet insistent beeping went off in his pocket, and Brad slapped a hand on his hip and swore, pulling out his phone and glancing at the message. "I'm sorry. Got to run."

She slipped off his lap and walked with him to the doors. "I really didn't expect you to do my job as well as yours," she pointed out.

"If you need me, call," Brad insisted, catching hold of her face and waiting until she dipped her chin in acknowledgement. Then he grinned, leaning in to kiss her hungrily.

It was far too easy to wrap her arms around him, and when he straightened and her feet left the ground, her tight hold and the grip he had on her hips kept them in contact. The solid length of his body pressed against her as he took the kiss deeper than before and set her entire body tingling.

When he put her feet back on the floor, she clung to him for a moment to get her balance.

A soft chuckle escaped him, and she tapped him on the chest as he let go. "Brad. Inappropriate behaviour in a church."

"Seriously. It's not my fault," he insisted before pointing a finger above their heads.

Hanna tilted back for a look where, sure enough, another batch of the dreaded mistletoe had been hooked to the ceiling in plain sight, right there in the entrance of the church. "Who hangs mistletoe in a church?"

"I'm not about to ask *why* when the *what* was so satisfying," Brad pointed out. He brushed his knuckles over her cheek and backed away. "Drive safe when you're done."

Then he was gone. A swirl of crisp winter air slid around her like an icy embrace, invigorating and refreshing and far too body-tingling.

Hanna went to work with a candle of hope burning in her heart.

It was one of those calls that would normally have caused Brad to breathe a sigh of relief. No buildings were threatened; no livestock was in the way. But the farmer who'd waited until past midnight to decide the brush pile he'd lit was burning oddly wasn't on Brad's favourite list at the moment. Not after he'd been pulled away from what was turning out to be a spectacular evening.

Of course the fire was burning abnormally. Unbeknownst to their father, the teenage boys in his family had hidden an entire box of fireworks at the base of the heap, planning to pull it out over the holidays when mom and dad were off visiting friends.

Dan Simpson cringed, ducking as if hiding from gunfire as another round went off behind them. "They'll be doing extra chores all holidays, trust me on that," he informed Brad.

"If you run out of dirty tasks to do here, send them down to the fire hall," Brad suggested. "We have lots of equipment that needs scrubbing."

A crack of amusement appeared in the farmer's annoyed exterior, and he pounded Brad on the shoulder. "I'll do that."

Brad waited with the truck for the pyrotechnics to exhaust themselves, dodging once when a flare escaped and shot straight between him and Mack.

Mack laughed, pulling himself out of the snow bank where he'd landed. "Never had to deal with fires like this back in Calgary."

Brad shook his head. "Fireworks aren't bad. It's worse when it's one of the old-timers' cabins and you discover they've got an ammunition stash under their bed. It was like walking into a war zone trying to get old Clancy Miller out of his bathtub before the entire house went up in flames around him."

Mack stared at Brad for a moment as if trying to figure out if he was lying or not.

Brad lifted a brow but didn't comment.

His friend shook his head. "The things people don't warn you about regarding small-town life."

They'd let the rest of the crew go, so it was just him and Mack who headed back to the station. They parked the truck and put their gear away, making sure everything was ready for next time the equipment was needed.

Brad glanced at his second-in-command, the two of them the

only paid full-time firefighters in the community. "What have you got planned for the holidays?"

Mack shrugged. "I'm working, so I'll be sticking around."

Stupid that he'd never thought of it before this moment, but it was the right thing to do. "Join us for Christmas Day."

"No can do," Mack offered with a grin as he put the final jacket in place. "I already have a date, and she's better looking than you."

Brad pulled himself to a halt. "Why didn't I know this? Who are you seeing?"

Mack's grin was a mile wide. "You didn't notice because you're a little obsessed and don't have room for anything in your brain other than Hanna Lane. And the answer to your second question is Brooke."

"Brooke the mechanic?"

"Yup."

Huh. Brad considered that for a moment before shrugging. "Good for you."

"Thanks for the vote of confidence. Not that I was sitting around waiting for you to bestow your blessing upon me or anything."

"Shut up."

"No problem. I need to hit the hay in case we get any other early New Year's Eve celebrations. Oh." Mack turned back in the doorway to the sleeping quarters where he was staying on-site. "The inspector already posted her report on the Jameson building fire—Hanna's place. Started from an electric short in the front law office. There was no vandalism or fault on anyone's part except the building owners."

"Perfect. Thanks for letting me know."

Brad took off for home, scrubbing down in a hot shower before collapsing onto his mattress.

The fire report wasn't something he'd been too worried about, because he knew Hanna wouldn't have done anything to cause the fire, but having her in the clear was like an extra Christmas present.

He wasn't sure what woke him, but suddenly, he was upright in his bed, listening carefully. If his brother was sneaking around—

His feet hit the floor, and an instant later, he was out in the hallway.

A whimper sounded from behind Hanna's door, and he didn't hesitate. He slid inside, marching across the room to the bathroom to turn on the light there so when she woke, she'd be able to see who he was.

She was thrashing hard, head rolling from side to side.

He stepped toward the bed. "Hanna."

Her arms shook, face crunched up tight as she curled into a ball, rolling on her side as if protecting herself.

It was possible he was about to get punched, but he couldn't let her keep suffering through her nightmare. He settled on the edge of the bed and laid a hand firmly on top of the blankets, pressing down on her shoulder. Speaking more forcefully, he said, "*Hanna*. You're having a bad dream. Wake up."

Her eyes popped open, and yes, her arm swung out, narrowly missing his face. He tensed, ready to spring away at the first sign of fear in her eyes as she focused on him.

Instead she snapped upright and threw herself into his arms, clinging to him. She quivered as she forced out the words. "Crissy's okay. The fire is over. Yes?"

He curled himself around her tighter, wanting to protect her from the past. "Crissy is sound asleep and snoring. The fire happened, but it's done. You're safe. You're both safe with me. You understand, sugar?"

Her head bobbed up and down against his chest. "My God, that was the most real dream I've ever had." She took a deep, still-shaky breath then curled up her fist and smacked it against his chest.

He grunted in surprise. "Hey. What was that for?"

She was still quivering, but now her voice held a touch of apology, and she tried to laugh. "You're the one who told me I was going to have some kind of panic attack. Thanks for setting up my nightmare."

Brad chuckled, rearranging his arms around her. "I'll take the blame."

Hanna tilted her head back, her hand sneaking behind his neck to stroke his head. "I was teasing. It's not your fault."

Sweet innocent. "I'll still take the blame. I've got broad enough shoulders."

Her gaze drifted down, eyes widening slightly as if realizing he had no shirt on, so the only thing between them was the thin layer of the T-shirt she wore—one of his, which gave him a kick of pleasure.

She had one hand around his neck and the other wrapped around his biceps. He liked her touch far too much considering when and where they were in this relationship. Which was why he fully expected her to maybe give him a kiss before scurrying to safety.

Instead she stroked him. A feather-light touch over his biceps and higher before coming back. Her gaze was fixed on her fingers as she explored, her hand drifting up then forward over his deltoid. Along the edge of his ribs.

Brad damn near held his breath as she leaned away far enough to expose his abdomen. He lost his breath in a solid gasp as her fingers trickled over his belly before sliding along his obliques.

"Hanna?" He swallowed hard. He wasn't even sure what he wanted to ask her except, dear God, he hoped she didn't stop.

She pressed her warm palm fully against his torso before lifting her gaze to meet his. "Stay with me."

This time he was the one to quiver. He wasn't going to turn her down, but damn if he'd let her go farther than she'd be happy with in the morning. "I'll stay until you fall asleep."

Confusion drifted over her expression.

He took control away, swinging the quilt back and sliding her to the middle of the mattress so there was room for him to join her. He settled on the bed at her side, keeping her tucked up against him, thighs brushing, torsos rubbing. He cradled her head on his arm and twisted until he could reach down the length of her.

A soft glow escaped from the bathroom and reflected in her wide eyes. He trailed his fingers over her chest, her heart pounding as hard as it had when he'd entered the room, but now it appeared, for a far better reason.

Hanna licked her lips, and his good resolve wavered.

"I'm going to kiss you, Hanna Lane, and there's not a single piece of mistletoe around."

Her lips quirked for a second. "Okay."

He leaned closer, pulling back as if he'd remembered something. "I'm going to touch you," he warned.

Her fingers snuck up his body, curling over his pectorals. "Okay."

Dear God, he was going to explode from the way she said that one word. He leaned in again, and this time, since he'd been good and asked for permission, there was no reason to go slow. No reason to start gentle, so he took her mouth and consumed her. Leaning against her because he could, pressing their bodies together yet somehow not rolling over her and pounding her into the mattress—

Civility barely held in place.

Her lips were so sweet, and the little sounds she made dragged up his spine as if she were using her nails on his skin.

He lowered a hand to her hip until he could slip under the edge of the T-shirt, rising slowly over her narrow waist. Past her ribs and up to cup one breast.

She gasped against his lips as he made contact. Brad pulled back so he could watch the expressions dancing over her face as he circled his hand against her tightening nipple.

He saw pleasure, desire, and the tiniest hint of fear.

It was that small reminder that let him regain his self-control to the point where he could give her what she needed right now. It wasn't going to be a sacrifice, not really. It was, however, going to make her forget all the worries she'd suffered over the past days.

That much he could promise.

10

She hadn't put it on her wish list for Christmas, but being in bed with Brad was definitely a present she'd wanted to unwrap.

Things were rolling awfully quickly, and yet she'd told him earlier about her concerns, and he'd done everything right. He hadn't mocked her or pushed them aside as foolish.

When she'd felt fear, his voice had cut through the terror. As the flames roared in her head, his voice had been the cool spray calming the fire and restoring order.

The heat, however, wasn't going down. Not. One. Bit.

Brad stared at her with desire in his eyes as his big hand rolled over her breast. Every part of her that had ever reacted with sexual interest had been plugged in and gotten fully charged over the past umpteen years.

His gaze drifted down to where he was playing, scraping his finger nails over her nipple until it tightened so hard she worried it might shear through the fabric of the T-shirt. Then that failed to be a concern because with a growl, he shifted position, tugging the material up far enough to expose both her breasts.

His expression went tortured, and he cursed softly.

Careful and slow—he was working too hard to not push her.

Hanna desperately wanted him to continue whatever it was he'd planned in the first place. She caught his head, rubbing her palms against the thin layer of rough hair, tugging him closer. He came willingly, plumping her breast before wrapping his lips around her nipple and sucking.

It'd been so long since anyone had touched her. There was really no way he could do this wrong, and a million ways to do it right.

He slid from one breast to the other, pressing kisses in the valley between them before licking the very tip of her nipple. He hummed happily, his expression clearly one of fascination.

It was addictive. So ego-stroking to see how happy he seemed as he touched her.

She was experiencing astonishing levels of pleasure, her skin alive and sensitive as he not only worshipped her breasts, but stroked his hands along her rib cage, drifting higher to anchor her neck as he briefly came back to kiss her.

Oh, those kisses. Forceful enough she couldn't escape, but gentle enough she didn't want to. He moved her under him until his tongue dipped into her belly button.

She shivered. "Brad."

"Close your eyes," he murmured. "You don't get to do anything right now but feel."

Which was a great concept except she was about to go into sensory overload. He tucked his fingers under her hips, big hands reaching forward so she was held in his embrace. His callused thumbs stroking her hipbones.

He played with the edge of her panties for a moment before peeling them away to leave her exposed from her chin down. He stared, that light in his eyes growing wilder, and when he reached up and laid a hand over her belly, Hanna quivered.

"So soft," Brad whispered, trailing his fingers to one side as he leaned in and pressed a kiss to where her panty line would have been. Then lower, to where curls covered her mound. "So soft and pretty."

She hadn't expected it, but when a giggle escaped, he glanced up, smiling. It took an extraordinary amount of strength for Hanna to speak, considering he was inches away from her sex and she was naked on the bed. Not a position she'd been in many times in her life.

"Pretty?"

He dipped his chin. "And tasty."

His words made her still, at least for the second before he stroked two fingers between her folds. Brad leaned in and lapped delicately. Then again, a brief touch before flitting away. Over and over until his teasing touch was too gentle and she was longing for more.

Which she got a second later as, with a growl, he adjusted position again, resting his elbows on the mattress and lifting her hips higher. Her knees fell apart, and she was spread like a butterfly as his mouth covered her completely. Shocking yet oh-so-right as his tongue did wicked things to her clit.

Her hips rose involuntarily, pressing down with her feet to get enough leverage. She forced herself against his mouth, and he laughed before putting his lips directly over her clit and sucking.

Stars danced in front of her eyes. She caught his head in her hands, rubbing her palms against the scruff. "That feels so good," she whispered.

"For me too." Brad lifted up, dropping her hips to the mattress but grasping her knees a second later to tilt them into the air. The motion rotated her hips skyward, opening her. No privacy, everything right there, spread open.

Whatever sense of embarrassment she should have felt had vanished, perhaps burnt up in the fiery dreams. Because, after glancing at her face to be sure she was onboard, his gaze drifted downward, lingering on her sex, on her breasts, returning to her face to make sure that she was happy—

No way was she going to deny either of them. "More," she begged.

She wasn't sure what exactly she was asking for, but she was good with anything he wanted to give. Which seemed to be kisses. He rocked forward to press one to her lips before moving lower to play with her breasts. His right hand slid along her inner thigh until he cupped her sex, pressing the heel of his hand against her clit with rotating pressure.

Brad lifted his head, his eyes hazy as he stared into her face again. "So many things I want to do," he admitted. "I could spend the day on your breasts, or pet your pussy for hours until you're limp and sated. I could touch you from one end to the other, and that's before I slip my cock inside you."

One finger copied his words, sliding through her folds slowly. Tracing around her entrance then pressing deep until his hand was hard against her.

His blue eyes watched. Judged. Made sure she was okay.

She wasn't okay. She was going to go out of her ever-loving mind.

"*Brad*," she said with as much warning as she could put into her tone. "Stop teasing," she begged.

His lips curled. "You think this is teasing?"

He kissed her again, but this time set his hand into motion. Pulling back, circling, pressing deep. He copied the same stabbing motions with his tongue, as if he was warning what came next.

The pressure between her legs increased as he added a second finger, slowly at first until her body spread to accommodate his thick digits. As her wetness coated them, he picked up the pace and sent her nerve endings into cardiac arrest.

Between one kiss and the next he was gone. His fingers stayed in place, moving and driving the pleasure higher. But he shifted position, and when he put his mouth back over her clit, Hanna moaned. She sucked for air, squirmed against him. Anything to try to get the last little bit she needed—

He increased the pace, driving his fingers deep, flicking his tongue relentlessly, and she was gone. Waves of pleasure streaked through her. They started at her core, wrapped around his fingers and spread like a net, pinning her to the mattress.

Brad rejoined her, kissing her again, and she tasted herself on his lips. A strange combination of her and him, intimate and sexual.

Her entire body quivered as he pulled his fingers from her body. Maybe she should've felt embarrassed, but she was so relaxed she was about to melt through the mattress.

He twisted her on the bed, wrapping himself around her. An all too apparent erection pressed against her backside.

Hanna stared up at him, hazy with sleep but wanting—

Wanting to make him as happy as he'd made her. Wanting to care for him as well.

Only before she could move, he tightened his arms around her and kissed the side of her neck, shushing her. "Sleep," he ordered.

He had her trapped, wrapped in a human blanket, protected and warm. Definitely relaxed from the sexual hormones flitting through her veins.

Hanna wasn't going to argue with him now, and when she woke in the morning in an empty bed, she really couldn't argue with him then either.

Something had changed. She still had her hesitations, and her worries, but overall, as she threw her legs over the edge of the bed and got up, Hanna knew they had moved to a new stage of their relationship.

Now she had to find a way to keep her courage up and follow through.

~

HE'D WONDERED if Hanna would retreat to shyness the morning after he'd touched her. Brad made sure to be out of her bed before she started to stir, partly to save her the embarrassment, and partly because he knew he was grumpy in the mornings and didn't want her to have to deal with him.

Although, truth be told, he wasn't very grumpy after what he'd gotten to do during the night. Being with her so intimately had happened eons before he'd expected, and he caught himself smiling at the strangest times throughout the day.

His coworkers noticed. Mack shook his head and threw wadded-up paper at him to get his attention more than once. "I'd tell you to stop looking so cheerful, but it's kind of amusing."

Brad made sure he whistled extra loud as he worked, ordering supplies for the coming year. Mack laughed in the background.

At home, Hanna offered him a sweet smile, but kept a proper distance whenever Patrick or Crissy were around. He followed her cues and made sure not to crowd her, but every night after Crissy went to bed and before Hanna headed off to work, he made sure to be available to steal a goodbye kiss.

He was getting adept at plotting where to stick the plastic mistletoe. He'd found a couple more clusters in the Christmas decorations box, and even though he'd scratched his hand on the batch he'd hidden in his pocket, looking for an opportune moment to set it in place, the red marks were a reminder of the sweetness of getting Hanna's full attention. Her arms would willingly wrap around his neck now as she'd step into his embrace and kiss him with rising heat.

He stayed out of her bed, though. He wasn't willing to rush that event even though his body wanted so much more.

The final day of school before the Christmas holidays arrived, and Patrick warned them in the morning to be ready for a surprise when they got home.

Crissy slipped from her chair and came over to Patrick's side. "Are you going to show us the reindeer?"

His father laughed and pressed a finger to his lips. "They're still resting," he said quietly. "But I have another way to get around. Wanted you to try a new adventure. You game?"

Crissy nodded then took Patrick's empty bowl and stacked it with her own, carrying them to the counter before rushing off to finish getting ready for school.

Hanna eyed Patrick with amusement. "Reindeer?"

He grinned. "Actually, if you're okay with the idea, I thought we could take the skidoos out for a spin."

That's why his father had been tinkering with the machines. Brad double-checked to make sure Hanna wasn't too horrified, but she was grinning.

"I haven't ridden a skidoo for years. Only, what size?"

The old man had this all figured out. "We've got big machines for Brad and I, but I also tuned up Connie's. It should be just the right size for you."

Hanna turned delighted eyes on Brad. "Can you come too?"

The faces focused on him all held the same question. Something strange and magical flipped in his belly. These were three people he'd come to care for so deeply. Making plans to do things with them—spending time together like they were a *family*...

"Of course." His words came out a gruff rumble.

They obviously thought the response was just him being his usual morning coffee-deprived self. Not because he'd had a deep, emotional revelation, like opening the perfect Christmas gift.

Patrick gave Hanna a refresher as Brad took Crissy for a slow first run through the trees. By the time they looped past the house, Hanna was ready to join them, an ear-to-ear grin in place. She was bundled up like an abominable snowman in her borrowed layers, but she looked delightful and perfect.

Little-girl laughter spilled into the air as he wiggled the sled back and forth, gently enough Crissy could keep a tight hold of his arms.

"Faster," she demanded.

He resisted the temptation to follow her order, at least until Hanna cut in front of him then sped away, glancing over her shoulder and sticking out her tongue.

They weren't racing at top speed but fast enough that when they finished, Hanna's cheeks were rosy, and the laughter in her eyes seemed to wrap around her body like a perfect set of Christmas lights, making her glow.

They rode the sleds for over an hour before they lost the light and put the sleds back in the barn.

Patrick was moving slowly, but he too wore a delighted grin. "It's been years," he told Hanna as they sat with cups of hot chocolate in front of the fire. "Connie always loved sledding. She was the one who taught the boys to ride."

Brad laughed. "I'd forgotten that. I remember you giving her trouble for driving too fast." He glanced at Hanna who blinked innocently and pretended she had no idea what he was talking about.

"You did well out there," Patrick told Hanna, giving Brad a wink. He'd noticed the racing as well. "When did you learn?"

She frowned for a moment before catching herself and forcing a smile back into place. "We used sleds at home to do chores."

"Mommy can do anything," Crissy announced proudly before breaking off into an enormous yawn.

Hanna stooped and scooped up her daughter, whirling her in a circle. "It's not time for bed yet, silly. We still have to eat supper." She gave her a kiss before putting her down on her feet. "Come on. Let's make something special for Mr. Patrick as a thank-you for the nice afternoon."

Crissy raced from the room, tugging Hanna with her. Brad watched them go, wondering if it would be completely inappropriate to stalk after them so he could continue to enjoy their company.

His father's chuckle pulled him from his musings. "You've got it bad," his dad teased.

Brad rose to his feet and offered his father a wide smile. "Correction. I've got it *good*."

Then he went and joined the girls in the kitchen so he could bump into Hanna as often as possible, her eyes flashing with amusement when she realized what he was doing.

Dinner was a noisy, happy affair, followed by games in the living room. When it was time to call it a night, to his shock, Crissy snuck her fingers into Brad's hand.

"I want you to tuck me in too," she whispered softly.

Brad glanced at Hanna who held still before dipping her head in permission.

He stood beside the bed, waiting, as Hanna pulled the blankets up then leaned in to kiss Crissy. "You need to get a good sleep," Hanna warned her. "There's no school tomorrow, but we've got lots of holiday things to do."

Crissy arranged her stuffed bear under her arm. "And you don't have to work?"

Hanna shook her head. "Holidays for me too. The whole time you're off from school."

Crissy sighed happily. "I liked the sleds. But I really want to see the reindeer."

Hanna stepped back, and Brad moved in, feeling slightly

awkward until Crissy held her arms up in a clear request for a hug. The little arms that wrapped around his neck turned his insides to absolute goo. And when she pressed her lips against his cheek before cuddling back under her blankets, shock and delight rippled through him.

"Good night, Mr. Brad."

"Good night, sweetie."

Crissy giggled. A sleepy sound as she closed her eyes and snuggled into the blankets. "I'm a sweetie because Mommy's sugar."

Brad held in his amusement, backing out of the room until he stood in the hallway with Hanna.

Unfortunately, her expression showed she didn't seem as pleased with her daughter's observant comment.

Only forward motion was allowed. He wasn't going to let Hanna backtrack on him. "You okay?"

She took a deep breath and lifted her eyes to his. "I forgot little people have big ears."

Brad stroked his thumb over her cheek. "I'm not going to hide what I'm feeling. And I don't think she's traumatized by the idea somebody likes her mommy."

Hanna wrapped her fingers around his wrist. Not taking his hand away, just holding him.

"No. She's—" Her gaze darted toward the ceiling and she rolled her eyes. "How do you keep doing that?"

The mistletoe he'd jammed against the ceiling before entering Crissy's room was right there, perfectly in position. "Santa likes me," he quipped.

Her lashes fluttered for a minute then she tilted her face without any further encouragement, waiting for him to lean down and kiss her.

Standing in the hallway, wrapped around each other, lips meshing, arms tangled. His entire body tightened, but somehow he pulled away after a decent amount of time, grinning at her flushed cheeks and the lights dancing in her eyes.

They stole back to the living room and visited with Patrick until his father once again fell asleep, the rocking chair in front of the fire a magnet to make him drift off.

Hanna slid to her feet. "Movie?"

He joined her. "You don't have to work at all over the holidays?"

She shook her head. "The only place I thought I'd have to clean was the church. The pastor called me this afternoon to let me know that after Christmas services, a group of them decided to volunteer to work the holiday season. He said it's my Christmas gift from the congregation—they're paying me, but I don't have to show up."

"Merry Christmas to you," he offered.

Her smile lit the room.

He'd left the remote control lying in his lap. She snatched it up, clicking the power on then holding the device out of his reach. "My pick."

Someone was feeling feisty tonight. "Maybe."

She flipped through Netflix, ignoring all of the shows on his watch list and going straight to the Christmas specials. Before he could tell which movie she selected, she'd hit play.

A romance with falling snow and impossible royal bloodlines popped on the screen.

Brad eyed her, playing up his disbelief. "Seriously?"

She stared straight ahead as if fascinated. "*Shhhh.*"

He searched for the control, but it was nowhere to be seen. Only, the smile on her face was twitching at the corners. Someone was being mischievous on purpose.

He laid a hand on her leg. "If I'm bored, I get restless," he warned.

Hanna glanced at him for a second before returning her gaze to the TV. "We can watch *Die Hard* tomorrow," she promised.

It was a good counteroffer, but he was still going to drive her crazy tonight. "Great."

He stroked his fingers up her leg, curling around the inside and down to the back of her knee. Teasing with his fingers over and over until she wiggled.

"*Brad.*"

God, he loved it when she said his name with that little combination of breathlessness and need.

He lifted his hand, turning toward her and draping his hand on the far side of her waist. "Don't mind me," he said, trailing his fingers up her side and under her arm.

She giggled, and he tickled harder. When she squirmed, rolling toward him, he took total advantage. He tugged her on top of his body, trapping her legs between his.

She pressed up on his chest, staring down. Hunger and happiness on her face.

He tickled her again.

Hanna burrowed against him, trying to escape. The movie was forgotten as they both took turns touching and teasing. Kisses stolen between heated touches. Innocent brushes of fingers followed by not so innocent—

The sound of Patrick's canes against the hardwood floor brought them both jerking back to reality. They scrambled apart as if they were teenagers instead of grown adults.

They were still about to be caught fooling around when they shouldn't be.

Hanna settled beside him, the two of them staring intently at the TV screen as Patrick poked his head in to say good night. "I'll see you two in the morning."

Hanna glanced over her shoulder. "Thank you for the loan of the sled. We had a wonderful time."

His father waved and disappeared down the hall. Hanna took a deep breath before glancing at Brad, mischief in her eyes. Then she wrapped her arms around his biceps and leaned against him, cuddled up and content.

He sat there, grinning at the screen for at least half an hour before he realized the same god-awful show was still playing. He didn't know where the control was, and he didn't give a damn.

It was a nearly perfect evening.

11

As they pushed through the doors into Buns and Roses, a veritable assault of Christmas scents struck Hanna full in the face. Cinnamon and ginger and rich peppermint, and she stopped to take a deep, appreciative breath.

Crissy tugged on her fingers, impatient to keep moving. "I see Emma," she said, bouncing on the spot. "And Sasha and Mary and Alicia."

Hanna helped her out of her coat. "I won't keep you from your friends."

"And you need to see *your* friends." Tansy's familiar voice was joined by her sister Rose and the other women Hanna had begun to gather with on a monthly basis. Friends Hanna knew had her back, and who cared deeply about her.

It felt wonderful to be in the midst of that kind of caring.

"I thought we were doing girls' night out," she teased.

"Today is girls' day in," Rose quipped. Her festive Christmas vest with shiny gold trim contrasted beautifully against her dark skin and hair. "Come on. We rearranged the shop so it's got a comfy corner for us to sit and gossip while the kids have room to play."

Tansy locked the door behind her, flipping the *open* sign to *closed* then brushing her hands satisfaction. "Now I can break out the spiked eggnog."

"One of the benefits of partying where you live," another of their friends teased. Brooke waved at Hanna before tightening her ponytail then patting the chair next to her. "Come sit by me. We haven't had a chance to talk for a while."

All of her friends were there except for Tamara who had been replaced by her sister Lisa. Not really *replaced*, but the cheerful woman was a welcome addition as she sat with the little girls and got busy helping them make Christmas decorations.

Ivy Fields settled in the chair on the other side of Hanna. "How are you?"

Wonderful? Excited? Quivering on the edge of something that seemed momentous? Hanna looked for the right words to share when she realized all of her friends carefully watching right now were thinking about the fire.

They weren't fixated, like Hanna was, on the fact that a certain oversized fireman was doing weird and wonderful things to both her libido and her heart.

"We're doing fine."

Brooke patted her arm. "You make sure you let us know if there's anything you need. I lost a bunch of stuff once when we had a fire in the shop. It was only a couple of boxes, but it was tough."

Hanna had been adding to her replacement list, but when it came down to it, the page was short. "We've never had a lot of things," she admitted. "Between a tight budget and it just being me and Crissy, the things that are most valuable to us are memories."

"That's how it should be," Ivy said with a gentle smile.

A couple of them got up to bring in snacks, but Ivy continued to study her until Hanna had to ask. "You seem to have something on your mind. Is something wrong at school?"

Ivy glanced over to where Crissy was happily playing with the other little girls. She reached into her pocket and pulled out an envelope, turning her body strategically so no one else could see. "I thought you should take a peek at this. It's Crissy's letter to Santa. Obviously, I don't have it anymore because we mailed it to him."

Hanna nodded in understanding then unfolded the page. It was her daughter's childish printing with some adult additions—Ivy's contributions. But as her gaze moved down the page, Hanna's heart began to pound.

Dear Santa,

Thank you for taking care of me during the fire. I know it's important to keep secrets, so I won't tell anyone that I know where you live. You are very nice, and thank you for sending Mommy someone to kiss.

I would like a daddy for Christmas. Emma said she asked for a mommy and got one, but it took a little while. I can wait, but I think Mr. Brad would make a good daddy, and Mommy likes him.

I really like your pancakes.

I hope you have a good trip on Christmas Eve.

Love, Crissy

She glanced up to see Ivy watching her with great curiosity.

Hanna folded away the page before the girls caught her with it. "Oh boy."

Ivy smiled. "Out of the mouths of babes."

There were so many things she wanted to say, but she wasn't about to defend herself, because she and Brad weren't doing anything wrong. But the idea Crissy was already wishing for more turned her hopes *and* her concerns a little higher.

She stuck with the safer topic to discuss. "Does she really think Patrick Ford is Santa?"

Soft laughter escaped her friend. "That's the part you're going to focus on? Okay, I won't tease you about getting kisses, or the fact that your daughter has chosen to act as matchmaker. Yes, I think she's pegged Patrick for Jolly St. Nick."

It didn't seem too dangerous an idea. "Do you think I need to talk to her?"

Ivy shook her head. "Out of all the people she could imagine to be Santa, Mr. Ford is one of the safest. He's not going to disappoint her with un-Santa-like behaviour, and he'd probably get a kick out of explaining how Santa can travel around the world in twenty-four-hours and still be home in his bed at a decent time."

Patrick *would* get a kick out of it. So would Brad, but the idea of sharing the rest of the letter with anyone else was out of the question.

She handed it back to Ivy. "Keep this for now, please?"

Ivy tucked it away without arguing then smiled. "I'm glad you have something good happening over the holidays."

Hanna ignored the question in her eyes.

Ivy leaned closer to make sure no one overheard them. "It's nice to have somebody to kiss."

That was very true.

Hanna enjoyed the party and the visit with her friends, but when they paused the party and all gathered together to lay a pile of presents at Crissy's feet, Hanna felt herself on the edge of tears.

Emma explained what was going on. "Since all your things are gone, you get extra Christmas presents. We gave up one of ours."

Lisa added the details. "All of the girls asked their moms and dads to give them one less thing, and then they got *you* something special."

Crissy's eyes were shining and she couldn't speak. The only thing that squeaked out was a heartfelt "Thank you."

"You get to open them right now," Tansy told her, dropping onto the floor to hand up the first package.

While Crissy worked on unwrapping her surprises, Lisa turned to Hanna and offered her an envelope. "We grownups did the same. We gave up one present, but instead of buying you things, we figured you should pick them yourself."

Happiness wrapped up in layers of shiny friendship flashed hard, and tears came to her eyes. "You guys are incredible. Thank you."

She strolled around the group, offering hugs and individual thanks to all her friends.

Crissy squealed as she opened a box and found a stuffed dog with floppy arms and legs. It wasn't exactly the same as the one she'd lost, but it was close enough to have come from the same litter.

As Crissy wrapped her arms around the present with joy in her eyes, Hanna had to turn her back and bury her face against Ivy, using her friend as a crying board.

Happy tears were still tears, and not something she wanted Crissy to worry about. Not today.

The afternoon passed quickly. When it was over and everyone was gathering their things to get ready to go, Hanna found herself looking out onto the street at a familiar face. Wondering where she'd seen—

It was Mark. Brad's brother. The man who'd surprised her.

She made sure Crissy was still busy before she slipped on her coat. Speaking quietly to Tansy, Hanna let her know she'd be a minute. "There's someone I need to talk to. I'll be right back."

She headed out the door, not completely sure what she intended.

Mark was staring in the window of the shop next door to Buns and Roses. It was a photography store that had sample portraits in fancy frames on display.

She followed his gaze to discover Mark was staring at a photograph of the Ford family. Her insides tangled up even more.

It was an old photo taken years earlier when Connie Ford was still alive. They were all dressed in jeans, leaning against a wooden rail fence that she recognized. The ranch's namesake lone pine tree stood proudly visible in the corner. Brad's hair was shoulder length, and he had an arm around his brother's shoulders. Patrick stood tall, his hair not the gleaming white it was now, but a salt and pepper shade. Connie smiled proudly, surrounded by her men.

Maybe Hanna was high on Christmas fumes, but suddenly all of her anger against Mark vanished as if someone had punctured a balloon. Didn't mean she was going to turn down a chance to give him hell, though.

She cleared her throat. "Mark?"

He twisted on the spot, his eyes widening as he stepped back. "You."

She thrust her hand forward. "Hanna Lane."

He glanced at her fingers then back up at her face as if suspicious of her motives.

It struck her as funny considering he was at least a foot taller than her. "I'm not going to hurt you," she deadpanned.

His lips twitched as he shook her hand briefly. "I'm Mark, although you already know that. Instead of saying hello, I'll say I'm sorry. I didn't mean to scare you. And I didn't mean to be rude."

"Apology accepted," Hanna told him. "But you were rude. Just to be clear."

He snorted. "Figures my brother would get himself a blunt-spoken girlfriend."

Having someone else call her Brad's girlfriend felt very, very good. "I saw you out here, and it's not my place, but I'm going to say it anyway. I don't know why you and Patrick are fighting. But it seems as if you're throwing away something good. You've got someone who cares a lot about you. Some *two*. Two people, that is," she explained herself. "Because I know Brad cares about you as well."

"When he's not threatening to hurt me."

She raised a brow. "You deserved it."

Mark made a face. "Blunt again. You're right. I did, but it just — you don't know—" He stomped away a couple steps before turning back. "It's not that easy."

"Good things never are easy," she said firmly, her gaze caught for a moment by her daughter. Crissy was dancing with her friend, hand in hand, holding the stuffed dog between the two of them. The toy's ears flapped as if it were laughing with joy. "Oftentimes, the most rewarding and valuable things take a lot of our energy and hearts, but they're worth it in the end."

Mark didn't say anything, but he was examining her face. He glanced in the window of Buns and Roses, his gaze lingering on Crissy. He turned back to Hanna as he figured out the relationship. He gave a brisk nod. "Thanks for not going ballistic on me, and I promise I won't sneak up on you like that again."

"I promise not to hit you with anything unless you deserve it," Hanna offered back. She looked him in the eye and realized she didn't have to lie. "It was nice to officially meet you. Merry Christmas."

"Merry Christmas," he repeated.

She went back into the warmth of the shop and caught hold of Crissy, holding on to her reminder of how much work it was for good things to happen, but how valuable it was at the same time.

She had her daughter, and she had something special developing with Brad. One step at a time. He'd been so patient and wonderful with her.

Maybe it was time for her to take a step closer as well. Something that would take effort on her part, but make *him* happy. The thought sent a shiver up her spine, but that wasn't a bad thing, she reminded herself. Anything worthwhile took hard work and might feel a little dangerous at first.

Now she had to look for an opportunity so she could take it.

Hanna and Crissy had returned from their afternoon party with a pile of presents and a boatload of joy shining in their eyes.

Patrick pulled Crissy into a game in front of the Christmas tree. Brad joined Hanna in the kitchen. She stood at the counter, flipping through the pages of his mother's recipe book.

She'd spent the afternoon with her girlfriends. He was pretty sure he'd been talked about at some point. He could hardly wait to figure out what had been said.

"What're you looking for?" he asked.

"Your father mentioned a cake your mom used to make during the holidays. I thought I'd put it together and sneak it under the tree for him."

It was impossible to resist. He stepped behind her, resting

one hand on the counter then reaching around her to flip to the page she needed. "That's a great idea."

She rotated in the circle of his embrace, and when she smiled up at him there was more than enough heat in her expression to make him happy. "Brat."

He chuckled. "I think you've forgotten my name."

Hanna pressed both hands to his chest, but instead of pushing him away, she slid her hands down his waist until they rested on his hips, holding him in place. "Trouble? Mischief?"

He wasn't sure what was going on, but he could work with this. "Sure."

After a quick peek around him to make sure no one was watching, Hanna went up on her tiptoes and offered her lips.

He smiled as he brought one hand up to cup her cheek. "I don't know what's come over you, but I like it," he murmured when the brief kiss was done.

Her lashes fluttered open. "Just following the rules," she insisted.

Hanna lifted a hand and pointed over their heads.

She must've crawled on the counter to hang the batch of mistletoe. It was taped near the top of the cupboard with what he knew was the only tape in the kitchen cupboard—plain, black duct tape.

Brad laughed out loud before her fingers landed on his lips, cutting off the sound.

They both stood and listened to see if his sudden outburst brought the attention of a certain little girl, but when the voices happily chatting in the living room stayed where they were, she slid her fingers away, pausing with a single one over his lips.

"Quiet," she ordered.

"Not a single peep," he promised before driving his fingers into her hair and tilting her head so he could kiss her again, this time hard and deep.

It wasn't enough. Not when, instead of responding shyly, she nipped at his lower lip and sent a spike of lightning through his body.

The next thing he knew, he'd lifted her, settling her butt on the counter. Sliding her knees open so he could press their torsos together. The aching ridge of his cock nestled against her soft center, and he tugged her hips forward so they rubbed, pressure building.

She'd pulled her lips from his and stared into his eyes as he rocked against her, panting lightly, both of them listening intently, ready to break apart on a moment's notice.

When the voices grew quieter, echoing from the mudroom, Brad decided he was truly getting absolutely nothing on Christmas Day because he was about to get a present he hadn't expected.

Sure enough, Patrick's voice rang from near the door. "We'll be back in a bit. The kittens need cuddles."

The door closed firmly before they'd had time to respond, and the silence in the house thickened.

An instant later Hanna had hold of his shoulders, fingernails digging in. She was the one to pull him closer and take his mouth by storm, tilting her hips against his in encouragement.

Glory hallelujah. Brad didn't think, he just took advantage of the moment and kept going. Accepting her kisses. The sweet, lustful press of her tongue teasing his. Grinding his hips against her in a decidedly non-innocent manner, lust building until she whimpered.

He slid one hand directly behind her to keep them connected, jerking her shirt from her pants and stealing his other hand under it to grasp her breast.

Hanna's head tipped back against the cupboards as a groan escaped her lips.

He wanted to strip her bare. He wanted to take her to his

room and bury himself in her body, but what he had was here and now. The clock ticking, her fingers digging into his shoulders.

She didn't want him to let go.

He put his teeth to her neck and nipped. Soothing it with a kiss before sliding up to an earlobe and doing the same thing there. Meanwhile, he slid his fingers under the soft fabric of her bra, teasing her nipple until it tightened. The entire time they rubbed together at that one dangerously combustible point.

"Brad. I'm close," she warned.

Him too, but damn if he was going to stop before she'd arrived.

He picked her up, shuffling two feet to the nearest wall and pressing her back against it so he could lean in harder. Applying more pressure to her clit as her eyes widened, and she scratched her fingernails down his arms.

He was holding on by a thin thread, ready to let go the second she did when, thank God, her legs tightened around his hips, squeezing in tiny convulsions as a breathless cry escaped her.

Brad lost it. Rocking against her now, hard enough the little Christmas knickknacks along the top of the wall rattled, making musical jingle bells sound faster than any street-side Santa.

It was wrong in so many ways, but that was the beauty of the perfect Christmas gift. It wasn't what you'd asked for, but it was exactly what you needed at that moment in time. Brad waited until the pressure built, pleasure tingling along his spine hard enough to make him want to scream.

Hanna cupped his face with both her hands, bringing their lips back together as he came. Hot and wet with a rush of endorphins that wiped out all worries about how dirty and out of control he'd been because she was kissing him. Holding on tight as if to squeeze the last dredges of pleasure from what they'd done.

When he pulled back, she looked as dazed as he felt, her smile decidedly on the naughty-list side.

"Dangerous vegetation, that mistletoe," he muttered.

Hanna laughed, and the amusement he'd held back earlier escaped, rolling up from his toes as he settled her back on her feet and offered her a delicate kiss. One that said he not only enjoyed what they'd done, but that he liked *her*.

He backed away before pinching the tip of her nose. "Have fun cake-baking."

Her gaze dropped momentarily to the front of his jeans where a noticeable wet spot had formed, and her cheeks went deep red.

"I need a shower," he informed her just to watch her embarrassment rise.

Then she surprised him again, offering a shy wink. "I enjoyed that."

So had he. And he was going to enjoy the next step even more, because *that's* what this latest escapade said. Hanna had made a decision to push the line forward, which meant his wish list was being answered. At some point, hopefully in the near future, they were going to make love, and he could hardly wait.

12

Hanna's daughter stood beside her at the breakfast table, all but quivering with excitement. "Please say yes," Crissy begged.

It wasn't only her daughter who turned puppy-dog eyes in her direction. Patrick had upped the ante to his most charming level of enticement as he sat kitty-corner to Hanna at the breakfast table. "Might be the only day this week nice enough to get outside, with that storm rolling in and all."

The only one who wasn't working his charm to convince her was Brad.

She smiled without thinking about it. He truly wasn't a morning person. In an attempt to not be outright cranky, he sat and silently sipped his coffee, refusing to participate in any conversation he could avoid until after nine a.m.

"Why am I the one who has to make the final decision?" Hanna asked, keeping her amusement out of her voice with difficulty. "If this were a democracy, since it appears Brad is abstaining, you'd already have more than fifty percent of the votes."

Patrick caved, looking slightly sheepish. "Everyone knows that a mother's vote counts double compared to the rest of us."

Brad snorted.

Nothing else, just a single snort, but that was more than his usual morning contribution, and suddenly Hanna had a deep desire to get up, storm around the table and throw herself into his arms. Maybe even tickle him until he laughed.

Although knowing him, tickles would probably change to kisses soon enough—and that was a line of thinking she needed to avoid.

Ever since she'd lost her mind in the kitchen a couple of days earlier, Brad had been careful to not push her, but he'd been watching closely. He was waiting, checking her for clues, and while she was really tempted to keep moving forward, the momentary pause had been good.

It gave her a chance to consider what was best, not only for now but for the future. For both her and Crissy.

It was too easy to fall into hopeful dreaming and wishful thoughts. Following through with what her body craved would be wonderful for the short-term, but considering what Crissy hoped to get for a Christmas present, Hanna knew she needed to take a few more deep breaths before committing any further.

Maybe this was right. Maybe Brad was the one for them, but she knew moving faster than they should might cause a world of hurt. She cared too much for Brad, and Patrick as well, to want that for any of them.

But this? The request before her right now was a kind of pleasure very much in line with good memories of the best kind.

She examined the two mischievous elves before her, one old, one young, and offered them an enormous, dramatic sigh. "Very well, if we *must* have a tobogganing party, I suppose—"

Patrick might've squealed louder than Crissy.

"Only you have to help make the calls to invite people,"

Hanna warned her daughter. "And you have to help set up everything *and* clean up any messes with me."

Crissy was already running off to grab the phone as Patrick pulled out a sheet of paper and began jotting down names.

Hanna met Brad's amused gazed. "You realize if you wanted to say no, now is too late."

"It's fine."

A whole two words. Wow, that was a record. "I'm going to remember this for the future," she warned him. "Anytime I want something from you, I'll just ask for it first thing in the morning."

The flash of fire in his eyes warned he was going to take her offer exactly the way he wanted to. "Please do."

He finished his drink and got up from the table, slapping a hand down on his father's shoulder before leaving the room.

Organizing the party took less than an hour. Shortly after noon, an assortment of cars and trucks were pulling up outside Lone Pine ranch. Once he'd woken up enough, Brad joined them and did more than his share to help get things ready.

No one came with empty hands, either. Little girls scattered with Crissy out to the barn to play with the kittens until it was time to load up the sleigh and head up the hill. Patrick watched with a contented grin as friends poured through his front door, pausing to say hello and wish him holiday greetings.

Tamara had made the trip and settled beside him as the action continued to flow into the kitchen.

Hanna paused to speak to her. "Glad you're feeling well enough to join in," she offered.

Her friend offered a weak grin. "If I disappear, don't take it personally. Just can't stand the thought of missing the girls' holiday excitement. I don't want all their memories of the coming baby to be about how sick I was."

Hanna planted her fists on her hips. "They're going to

remember their mama took good care of the baby even before it came out of her belly. Kids are resilient," Hanna reminded her.

"Good point." Tamara offered a sincere hug. "Thanks."

By the time everyone had been loaded onto the sleigh, there was enough of a crowd that Walker and Caleb mounted up on a couple of extra horses. Patrick sat with the children on the hay bales. Hanna got squeezed between Tamara and Brad, her legs tight against his. When he put both reins in one hand and slipped the other behind her back, it took her at least three minutes to start breathing normally again.

She was in his arms, exactly where she wanted to be—no more lying to herself. The idea still scared her to death, but she ached for his touch, for more of his kisses and his caring.

He pulled the sled to a stop beside the old mountain cabin and everyone unloaded, setting up sleds and taking picnic baskets into the wooden structure. They got the stove going and hot cider warming on the surface, and for the next hour or so children flew up and down the hill with the adults helping pull the sleds to the top again.

It was pleasure of a most innocent sort, filled with happiness and a sweet joy. Hanna took the time to examine her friends' faces, thrilled to see they were enjoying themselves thoroughly.

Even Tamara, who'd retreated to a bale tucked into the shelter of the cabin. Her daughters were alternating sitting with her and sliding, and when Caleb strode over and knelt by her feet, stroking her cheek with visible love in his touch, Hanna had to look away.

Spotting Brad staring at her did nothing to calm the pounding in her heart. She wanted—

"Mommy. Come play," Crissy demanded, catching her hand and pulling her into the delighted bevy of little girls. Hanna snuck a final peek at Brad. He winked at her, and then she was caught up in Crissy's laughter.

Snow began to fall. Big fluffy flakes at first, festively covering everything like the best of homemade holiday decorations, before coming down thicker and thicker. Hanna whirled on the spot, the happiness inside her spinning free. She caught snowflakes on her tongue with her daughter as Sasha and Emma and Crissy's other friends made snow angels.

It was a situation far removed from fear and decisions and momentous events—and Hanna wanted it to go on forever.

HE'D BEEN WATCHING HER. No, he'd been *staring*, unable to look away as she danced with her friends and the children, sheer joy in every step.

Someone cleared their throat.

Brad shook himself, glancing to the side to see Walker eyeing him, amusement on his face.

"Don't bother saying it," Brad warned.

"You don't want to hear that the hot chocolate is ready? When did we outlaw talking about holiday drinks?"

Brad took a step closer and let their shoulders bump, hitting Walker hard enough the other man spun. The snow under his feet shifted and his feet flailed. He landed on his ass in the snow.

Even as he laughed Walker rolled, taking Brad's feet out from under him, the two of them wrestling like they were children again, out in the schoolyard in those early elementary years.

Of course, the instant they started roughhousing, the kids found it far too entertaining to stay away, piling on top until there was snow down the back of Brad's collar and Walker had piles of the white stuff on both shoulders.

"Inside to warm up," Hanna sang out. "Come on, girls. And *boys*," she said, smiling directly at Brad.

Crissy and the rest of them took off with squeals, pigtails and scarves flying as they slid back into the warmth of the cabin.

Walker held out a hand and Brad grasped it, the two of them leveraging each other to vertical. "Looks as if someone's made herself at home."

Brad batted at Walker's arm, pretending to knock the snow from him. "Don't you have someone special you're supposed to be off bothering?"

"I do," Walker said with a satisfied grin, glancing at Ivy who was bundled up head to toe, her puffy blue coat shining like a bit of sky against the pristine white. "I'm happy for you," he offered.

"Don't get too excited," Brad warned. "Things are going well, but I'm not getting ahead of myself."

Walker leaned in close, sliding an arm around Brad and patting him firmly on the shoulder. "I hear you, but I think you're pretty much in a good place. Of course that's why, since Hanna doesn't have anyone here to do this on her behalf, I'm just going to warn you now. If you do anything to hurt either one of those girls, Ivy has given me specific instructions to drag you into the arena and tie you under a bull."

"Women are so bloodthirsty," Brad complained. "They look innocent, but they're prone to violence far quicker than we are. Hanna gave my brother a bloody nose. Walloped him with her brush."

His friend laughed, guiding him toward the cabin. "Good. I like to hear that she can take care of herself."

Brad did too, but what he really wanted was to be the one caring for her. Not because Hanna was incapable but because something deep inside him longed to care for them both.

They'd set up a fire pit outside the cabin, logs placed around for seating. Walker offered Ivy a sly wink before leading the group in singing Christmas carols. As Hanna settled at his side,

Brad wondered how much longer he was going to have to be patient.

When Crissy wandered over, slid into his lap, and rested her head on his chest, Brad found it hard to breathe.

Especially when Hanna glanced upward, her gaze drifting over her daughter and up to his face. She was thinking hard, sort of smiling and sort of not, but when she tucked her mitts under his elbow and leaned her head against his arm, something went *pop* inside him, as if one of the old-fashioned holiday dinner crackers had gone off. Tightness relaxed as hope swept in.

Across the fire, Walker and Ivy were both smirking, other friends as well looking at them—he, Hanna and Crissy—with approval.

Honest truth, Brad wanted something special for Christmas, but he knew damn well he didn't always get what he wanted. Wanting something didn't make it so.

He knew that from a couple years earlier when his mom had gotten sick. It didn't matter how many Christmas wishes they'd made, she'd still faded from them, leaving his dad alone after so many years together.

It didn't seem to matter how often he'd wished for his brother to stop fighting and come back home. And it hadn't changed things at all to wish that his father hadn't been hurt. Brad was old enough to know that sometimes life didn't work out the way he wanted.

He glanced down at the woman at his side and at the little girl in his arms, and in spite of knowing the truth, it didn't change a thing. Sometimes the world was cruel and bad things happened. Sometimes he didn't get what he wanted. But the things that really mattered—the ones that absolutely had to come true—he'd fight for them, no matter what.

Which was why he was going to do everything he could to make *this* moment a reality forever.

13

The whole group made it back to Lone Pine before the snow really started coming down. Everyone headed to their vehicles, no excuses needed as they hurried to get off the roads before they became impassable.

"Light fluffy flakes, and they're still treacherous," Tansy complained to Hanna, slipping her feet into her boots and getting ready to leave with her sister.

Brad's phone had gone off a moment earlier, and he was talking in the background, probably being summoned on a call. He joined them, pulling on his jacket and frowning outside at the vehicle the girls had arrived in. "I have to head into town. I'll give you a ride," he suggested. "You can pick up your car tomorrow once the plows have been out."

They accepted his offer, giving Hanna and Patrick hugs before slipping out.

Brad dipped his chin at his father then leaned in and kissed Hanna quickly. "I gotta run."

She didn't even have time to be embarrassed that he'd kissed her like that in public. Everyone was scurrying around, and they went from a houseful of people to only her, Patrick and Crissy in less than fifteen minutes.

"I think that's a new record," Patrick said when she mentioned it. "But it makes sense. Arriving home before the roads are impassible is a good idea." He moved slowly as if in pain.

"Can I get you something?" she asked.

Patrick hesitated before offering a reluctant nod. "I wouldn't have traded being out there for anything, but I'd better take something or I won't sleep, and I'll be in worse pain tomorrow."

She put on the kettle then ran to get the painkiller from his locked bathroom cupboard. Patrick took the medication then settled in front of the fire. He closed his eyes, and as he relaxed, the deep lines of pain on his face eased slightly. Hanna grabbed a knitted throw off the couch and tucked it over him, a sense of connection she hadn't expected filling her.

Crissy thought Patrick was Santa Claus, and they would have to deal with that at some point. What was true was that the older man had become more than just a casual friend over the past week.

Crissy had vanished the instant her friends had left. Hanna assumed that she'd gone to play with her new toys, only after getting Patrick settled, she went to check and Crissy wasn't in her room.

Hanna stood quietly, heart pounding as she tried to figure out where her little girl had gone. She checked in her bedroom, both bathrooms, the craft room, and on the off-chance, she even opened the door to Brad's room.

Nothing there except a neatly made king-size bed.

It was only when Hanna thought to look for boots that she realized Crissy must've snuck out to the barn. The girls had been playing with the kittens before the trip up the hill, and Crissy had probably wanted to go say good night to them as well.

She pulled on her coat and made her way out to the cozy shelter, passing stalls for the horses who were happily munching on their late dinner. Even though their company had left in a rush, all the cowboys had paused, taking care of the horses thoroughly before leaving them warm and happy for the night.

She found Crissy sitting cross-legged with the kittens in her lap, her face streaked with tears.

"Sweetie, what's the matter?" Hanna asked in a panic, checking to see that there were no obvious signs of hurt.

Crissy's voice was a wobbling cry. "We forgot Blackie."

Hanna didn't understand. "You forgot Blackie where?"

Utter misery looked up at her. "We snuck Blackie with us, up to the cabin. He was in my pocket on the trip there. I thought Emma brought him back, but she couldn't catch him and then she rode with her daddy and I was on the sled, and she couldn't tell me until we got back and now he's all alone."

After the joy of the day, her daughter's fear and sadness melted Hanna's heart. "The cabin is warm. Blackie will be okay."

"But not when it gets cold." Tears slid down Crissy's face. She was crying so hard she barely made any noise.

"It's okay. We'll find a way to make it okay," Hanna promised, slipping the kittens from Crissy's lap and back with their mama before picking up her little girl and heading into the house.

"I want to call Brad," Crissy whispered. "He'll make it better."

But Brad was gone on a fire call. Still, Hanna knew he'd want to be told. "I'll phone him right away."

She stood in the mudroom as Crissy raced off, waiting with faint hope until the line went to Brad's voice mail.

Something else had to be done.

Crissy had already informed Patrick what was wrong. The old man had made his way into the kitchen, resting uneasily at the table with concern in his eyes. "I'll go get the little thing."

Hanna placed a hand on his shoulder and stopped him from rising from his chair. "You'll do no such thing."

"But Mommy—"

"But Hanna, girl—"

She stilled them both with a stern glance. "This is just as important to me is it is to you, but I'm not about to let Mr. Patrick go do something dangerous. You took enough painkiller to put an elephant to sleep," she told him sternly. "Exactly how do you think you're going to get to the cabin and back without hurting yourself?"

He sat back heavily in his chair, one of his canes clattering to the floor, echoing like a gunshot. "Oh. That."

She folded her arms over her chest. "Yes, *that*."

Crissy pressed her face against Hanna's belly, utter misery in her voice as she spoke. "Is Blackie going to die?"

Hanna stroked a hand over her daughter's head. "Of course not. Only we need to be smart and make an emergency plan. Sometimes we have to move fast, like when Mr. Brad got you out of the fire. But most of the time when something goes wrong, we slow down and think hard so we can make a *smart* plan. Let's work on that, okay?"

She pulled out a chair and lifted Crissy into it before slipping to the counter and making cups of hot cocoa. Even though she didn't want it, she knew the hot drink was a good idea for her as well.

Patrick patted Crissy on the shoulder gently. "Your mom is right. I know that rule, but I kind of forgot."

Crissy looked up at him before assuring him sweetly, "Worrying about a kitten makes it hard to follow rules."

"So it does, little missy, so it does."

Hanna placed herself opposite them, waiting until Crissy took a few deep swallows. Then she laid her hands on the table and listed options. "Brad is gone to work, and while I know he can help us when he gets home, we should make plans in case that doesn't happen for a while. Patrick, how long do you think the cabin will stay warm enough that Blackie will be fine?"

He gave it deliberate thought before speaking slowly. "At least until the morning. With the snow coming down, it's not that cold. The place is well insulated. I've banked the stove in the evening and had it shirtsleeve temperature still at noon the next day in weather like this."

"Then there's no need to rush," Hanna pointed out. "In the morning, when Brad's home, we'll ask if he can take you up to rescue Blackie."

Crissy's shoulders relaxed as if all the fear had gone out of her. Only she stared at Patrick with begging in her eyes. "Are you sure you can't send Rudolph?"

The older man glanced at Hanna with concern before shaking his head and motioning for Crissy to come climb into his lap. "You know that Santa is magic, right?"

She nodded slowly, fingers reaching up to brush his beard.

He smiled, laugh lines crinkling at the corners of his eyes. "One thing Santa does because he can't be everywhere, is that he shares his special magic with people. It's not the kind of magic that can make reindeer fly, but the kind that makes people happy inside. It's special magic that helps them do things to make others happy. That's how Santa can get so much done even though he's just one man. He gets other people to be stand-in Santas for him."

Crissy's eyes widened with understanding. "So, you're not Santa, but you *know* Santa?"

Hanna was holding her breath, wondering how on earth Patrick was going to keep this from exploding into a terrible situation.

She should have known that the smart, caring man could handle it.

He tapped Crissy on the nose before putting his finger

against his lips as if about to share a secret. "Santa gets around. Chances are you've met him too, and no one who has ever met him comes away without being changed. You're right. I'm not Santa, but I'm very well acquainted with the old rascal, and all the things that are important to him are important to me. Including little Blackie. I don't have any magical reindeer that can bring him home, but between my son and your mom, I know everything will be fine."

Crissy glanced at Hanna. Speaking in a whisper as if Patrick wasn't even sitting there. "Have *you* met Santa?"

Hanna thought back to the people who had helped her when she'd been homeless and pregnant. To the people who'd been there for her when she'd been struggling as a single mom. To the new friends who had given so joyfully to her and Crissy in the past days.

To Brad and Patrick who had opened their home, and their hearts, to needy friends.

"Yes," Hanna assured her. "I know lots and lots of Santa's helpers."

Crissy lifted her hand and pointed with her thumb over her shoulder at Mr. Patrick, raising her brows as if asking for confirmation.

Hanna leaned forward. "Definitely Santa's helper."

Her daughter took a deep breath and leaned her head against Patrick's chest. A look of amazement came over the old man's face as he tentatively cuddled her in.

"I thought Santa's helpers were called elves," Crissy said, her voice tired after the worry and excitement of the day.

Patrick chuckled, the sound so much like Brad's it made something stir inside Hanna. Another reminder of the connection growing between all of them. Something warm and rich—a lot like what family was supposed to feel like.

The callout hadn't been from the Heart Falls district, but three zones away, closer to Crowsnest Pass. As fire chief for the district, he had to travel farther when it was called for, but it sucked when it was one of these distant emergencies at a time he'd hoped to stay close to home.

Worst thing was moving deep into the country meant losing cell coverage nine times out of ten, and today was no exception. Brad was unable to phone Hanna and Patrick to let them know where he was.

He shook hands with the volunteer team to call it the end of a successful mission then drove for over an hour in the darkness before the sun began to lighten the sky. Long, dark days were the rules in December, but between the darkness and the heavy snow that continued to fall, Brad had inched forward instead of rushing home the way he wanted.

He got up the road to Lone Pine with difficulty, even his 4 x 4 fighting against the deep snow piles that had built since the night before. He was smoky and tired, and absolutely thrilled to push open his front door and walk into the warmth.

Being assaulted by a small child who wrapped her arms around him then burst into tears was the last thing he'd expected.

He stooped and picked her up, petting Crissy on the back. "Hey, sweetie. What's this all about?"

Patrick's canes echoed closer, his father's face drawn with concern as he joined them in the hallway. "You didn't check your messages."

Brad shook his head. "I've been out of range and figured I should just come home."

Crissy caught him by the face and forced him to look at her. "Mommy went to save Blackie, but now she's going to be lost in the storm."

A rush of adrenaline through his system sent every nerve to high alert. "What did Hanna do?"

Patrick held up a hand to Crissy. "Slow down, little missy. Let me explain, okay?"

She wiggled until Brad put her down, rushing into the kitchen as Patrick hurried to fill Brad in. "Seems the girls smuggled one of the kittens out on our tobogganing trip yesterday, and the teeny thing got left behind at the cabin. We waited until this morning, but Hanna insisted she'd better go get it before the weather got any worse. That was an hour and a half ago. She should have been back by now."

Brad held his curses, quickly glancing out the window at what he already knew. "The snow is coming down harder than it was before."

"She insisted she was comfortable riding the sled, and she knows the way. She must've had engine trouble or something."

It made sense, but Brad was kicking himself that he hadn't been there to help before Hanna had gone into the wilderness on her own. He hurried down the hallway to his room to grab a few things. "What was she wearing?"

"She's warm. I made her put on Connie's sledding gear, and she took some supplies just in case." Patrick pointed back down the hall. "We put together some more food, so you go ahead and find her. Crissy and I will be okay until you bring her back."

Brad gathered everything he thought he might need, stuffing a duffel bag full with extra warm clothing and emergency gear for if the worst had happened.

He marched into the kitchen to find Crissy making more sandwiches. Her face was set as if she was determined not to cry as she spread peanut butter carefully.

She spoke without looking up at him. "This is my fault," she whispered.

Brad went to his knees in front of her, catching hold of her shoulders and making her look into his eyes. "Maybe you shouldn't have taken the kitten to the tobogganing party, but accidents happen. That's no one's fault, and I don't want you blaming yourself for something like a snowstorm. Do you really know how to control the weather?"

She shook her head, eyes filled with moisture. "But Mommy's not here, and that's my fault."

Brad itched to get outside, but Hanna would've insisted this was more important. "Your mommy is a grownup, and she makes her own decisions. If she went after Blackie, it's because she thought it was the right thing to do. Just like I'm a grownup, and I'm going to do what I think is right."

"You're going to go save Mommy and Blackie?"

"I'm going to go give them a hand," he corrected. "I don't think they need saving. I think they just need a friend."

Crissy put her arms around his neck and squeezed tight. "I'm glad you're our friend."

"I'm glad too," he said, squeezing her back and soaking in strength from the little girl's friendship to chase away some of his fears. Then they stacked the sandwiches together and added them to the food supply Patrick had already prepared.

The two of them accompanied him to the barn where he got the sled ready. Crissy pressed a kiss to his cheek before going back to Patrick's side.

"You take care of my dad," Brad told her sternly. "You tell him to make you grilled cheese sandwiches for lunch. And if I don't get back with your mom today, that means we're just being safe. You go to sleep on time so that Santa can come, okay?"

Crissy slipped her hand into Patrick's. "Okay."

"Do whatever you need to stay safe, and don't worry about us." Patrick ordered him. "We'll be fine."

It was like driving into the thickest fog imaginable. The only thing Brad had in his favour was he knew the land from having travelled over it since he was a little boy. Plus, his mom had trained them to use the rolling lines of gullies and hills to follow instead of relying on trees—she'd warned them there'd be times when they might not be able to use their vision, but they could know where they were.

She'd taught them there were times when getting home might be impossible, but you could still be safe. Hunker down, stay with the sled.

It was the only thing he was afraid of—that Hanna had gone off the trail somewhere and he'd miss her.

But his mom had also said to plan for the worst and hope for the best, so Brad headed straight to the cabin, putting aside the rest of his emergency plans until he knew for sure they were needed.

He came over the second-to-last rise when the scent of wood smoke struck him, strong and deep, and in spite of not being able to see anything, his fears settled somewhat. Someone was in the cabin, because the smoke was thick and new, not a smolder lingering from the day before.

He parked beside her sled, dragging the emergency supplies with him as he marched up on the porch. Stomping his feet and brushing the snow off his shoulders before he opened the door and peeked in.

The one-room cabin glowed with soft candlelight, flames flickering in the glass front of the airtight stove. Hanna straightened from where she'd been sitting in front of the fire, and a small black cat jumped from her lap and stalked lazily across the floor.

Relief tangled with joy, and he dropped his bags to one side so he could push the door shut, throwing the bolt against the rising wind.

Hanna met him halfway across the floor, pressing herself

against him and grabbing on tight. Brad squeezed her, closing his eyes and letting his heart rate return to normal.

When he opened his eyes, it was to discover the strangest setup in the corner of the room. A chair rested on top of a box on top of the kitchen table, all of it like a strange set of stairs rising toward the roof. "You've been redecorating."

Hanna shifted back in his arms. Her cheeks were rosy, and she was covered from head to toe in warm flannel. "I had a few troubles retrieving Blackie," she explained.

He eyed her contraption a little closer as he removed his boots and snowy gear. She took things from him, hanging snowy garments on hooks and moving quietly as the fire crackled in the stove.

"I take it the ungrateful creature wasn't waiting patiently by the door for you to rescue it?"

Hanna shook her head. "How's Crissy? She must be scared to death."

"She's fine. Patrick talked her down. She sent you a million peanut butter sandwiches so you wouldn't starve." He closed the distance between them. "You scared me too," he whispered. "I can't believe you came out here to rescue a kitten."

"You would've done the same, and you know it," she told him briskly, placing her hand over his. "I was just catching my breath before heading back."

The wind chose that moment to rush up, stronger than before. It rattled the windowpanes and sent a long, low whistle through small cracks in the chinking between the logs.

"We're not going anywhere," Brad informed her. "The chance of getting lost is too high."

Hanna went to the door and tugged it open, the icy wind swirling around her and flipping her hair hard. Brad reached past her to push the door closed, setting his shoulder into it as a gust nearly tore it from him.

"It wasn't like that when I rode up," Hanna told him. "I wouldn't have gone out, not even for Blackie, if it'd been like that."

Her reassurance melted the final bit of fear inside his chest. "Good."

Her gaze dropped over him, pausing on his cheek, and she stepped closer, running her thumb over his skin before pulling back to show a trace of soot. "Did everything turn out okay?"

"Other than I need a shower, yes."

It was as if the thought hit both of them at the same moment. He'd warned her they weren't going anywhere, not until the storm passed. They had food and warmth, and for the first time since they'd begun seeing each other, they were utterly alone. No one was going to walk in on them. No little girl would be knocking on the door to interrupt—

Hanna turned away, pacing to the counter where she pulled the largest pot from the draining rack where it had been left after the party. She came back, her face poker straight. "Before you get too settled in, I guess we'd better start melting snow."

He pulled his coat and boots back on and slid outside, bringing in extra firewood while he was at it. Every time the door opened Hanna was there, working at his side.

Neither of them said anything about what potentially could happen. But they were thinking about it, both of them, awfully loud. Brad knew no matter how much he wanted her, unless she made a move, he wasn't going to push her.

It was up to her now. All up to her.

14

It was less than twenty-four hours until Christmas, and Hanna wanted nothing more than to give Santa a firm talking to.

Or maybe she should scold herself. She should know better than to casually make wishes like *if only I could be trapped alone with Brad Ford for a while.*

Because it had happened. They were trapped, all alone in a remote cabin that was warm and getting warmer.

The scent of wood smoke wasn't just coming from the fireplace but drifting from the gentle giant who stood at the table organizing the food supplies they had between them. He'd loaded the woodpile to overflowing, then carried two enormous stock pots to the surface of the stove, both of them packed solid with snow.

After removing his outdoor gear, shaking the fresh snow off and hanging it to dry, he'd helped her disassemble her makeshift ladder.

A rumbling laugh escaped him as he eyed the distance to the

roof. "How did Blackie get up there in the first place?" he asked with amusement.

"He must be one of Santa's and knows how to fly," Hanna said somewhat grumpily, because discovering the kitten wasn't going to cooperate had been a challenge she hadn't expected to face on top of everything else.

And now Brad was trying hard not to look at her, which in a way made it nice for her because she'd settled in the chair by the fire again, with a clear view as he worked at the table.

He'd pushed up his sleeves, and his strong forearms were marked with faint lines of soot. Once again the words rose to her lips to suggest he wash up.

But that would mean he'd be taking off his clothes, and Hanna didn't think she was strong enough to simply turn her back and pretend he wasn't there. To pretend she didn't want to watch as he stripped everything from his strong body.

It would take more strength than she had to deny that what she wanted was to strip down with him and take this relationship to the logical next step.

She tucked her legs in tighter, wrapped her arms around her knees and stared into the fire, letting her racing thoughts circle again and again until peace slid into place. It seemed impossible to focus on the gold and red flames and keep the tension twisting inside. And as the warmth stroked her arms and Brad settled into the chair beside her, Hanna realized her biggest fears weren't about him.

It was still the past shaking her foundation. It was still worries that, if she took another step, he might turn around and strip her heart away. Because there was no lying to herself about this—it wasn't just physical need between them.

Her heart was involved.

Hanna turned and deliberately examined him, thinking of everything that made Brad who he was. His ready smile, the way he moved his big body so intentionally, turning himself into a protective wall at a moment's notice.

Strong hands that he'd used to cradle Crissy carefully, the same hands that had sent his brother reeling and had also brought her pleasure—

The things she knew about him, she admired. He wasn't the boy who'd slept with her then broken her heart. He wasn't her family who'd deserted her when they should've been supportive.

Brad was solid, not just in body but inside as well, and whatever fate had brought them to this point, it was time for her to let go of the past and embrace her future.

The lid on one of the pots rumbled as the water came to a boil, and Hanna rose to her feet, ignoring the question in his gaze as she pulled together the things she needed. She gathered a cloth she'd found in one of the totes and a washbasin that she balanced on the table beside the wood-burning stove. She placed a couple of scoops of cold water in first before adding ladles from the stove until the tub was the perfect temperature.

Hanna took a deep breath then turned to face him. "Take off your shirt," she ordered.

Brad went still. Motionless as he looked her over from top to bottom. "Hanna?"

Announcing her intentions was intimidating beyond belief, and yet he deserved to hear it. She pulled in her bravery and stepped between his knees, reaching to undo the buttons of his shirt. "You smell like a fire pit," she told him bluntly.

Amusement flashed in his eyes. "This isn't an uncommon thing with me."

"I've noticed. I don't mind, most of the time, but I don't want our bed sheets coated with soot."

He caught her wrists in his hands, preventing her from pushing the shirt off his shoulders. "*Hanna.*"

This time her name came out somewhere between a promise and a plea.

She pushed against him, and he released her immediately, wiggling his shoulders to help her strip away the first layer. Reaching down, their hands bumped together as he helped pull the T-shirt from his body.

Naked from the waist up, he adjusted forward in his chair, opening his thighs wider to give her room to step closer as she brought the washcloth to him. She wiped his face clean, passing the cloth over his head and down his neck. Hanna turned back to dip the cloth in the water, wrung it out, then touched it to him again. She washed his shoulders, his arms, over his broad pectorals and down his ribs. His breathing picked up, chest moving under her touch.

His erection pressed to the front of his jeans, thick and ready.

She dipped the cloth again, thankful for the momentary breaks between touching him because she was on fire with need. Moving toward him instead of walking behind him, she reached around to wash his back, her gaze frozen on his face as he watched her intently. His bright blue eyes were filled with need.

Hanna gave the cloth another rinse before washing his arms, his forearms, stroking the soft fabric between his fingers.

The water had cooled, so she added another scoop of hot, and bracing herself to turn back, she motioned him to his feet.

He rose, towering over her, and yet she felt as if they were perfectly even, equals in desire and need and want.

Hanna reached for his button and undid his pants.

It was one of those moments where Brad worried if he made a single sound he would somehow disrupt the magic. That Hanna's trembling hands as she opened his jeans and helped push them off his hips would vanish, and this would all turn out to be some kind of feverish, lust-filled dream.

Only as he helped strip his pants away and she gasped softly, turning back to grab her washcloth, he knew the magic was strong enough to last.

She'd decided, and he was so very thankful.

The warm cloth stroked his thighs. Hanna's eyes widened as she touched him and washed his legs while she worked around the territory still covered by his briefs. It was cute to see her pointedly ignore his cock even as the rigid length blatantly attempted to escape its confines.

Cute at least until she paused in front of him, slowly lifting her eyes to meet his. "Take them off," she ordered, as bold as any drill sergeant.

No hiding now. His cock bounced back to near vertical, so hard from anticipation he ached. When she soaked the cloth again and wrapped the fabric around his length, rubbing carefully, Brad swore softly.

If anything she just stroked harder.

"You'd better be done soon," he warned, the words rumbling out barely comprehendible.

Hanna laughed, the sound lightness and joy, and she stepped away, her gaze far bolder than he expected.

When she lifted her hands to the bottom of her shirt and pulled her sweater over her head, his heart beat with the *pom-pom* of a drum.

Sweet innocence stripped in front of him.

She folded her sweater carefully then placed it on a chair before she shimmied out of her pants. When she was down to nothing but a plain white bra and underwear, feet clad in grey woolen socks she paused, hands hanging by her sides.

"Dear God, Hanna, you're killing me."

She turned on the spot, slowly reaching behind her and

removing her bra before facing him again. Breasts high, nipples tight. Cheeks flushed as she tucked her thumbs into the edge of her panties and pushed them down her legs, and then she was naked except for the socks.

His brain was three seconds from going off-line for good, but before he had a total mental meltdown, a moment of panic rushed in.

He lifted a finger in the air. "Don't move," he ordered.

Brad rushed across the room to where his bag was, desperately digging into the side pocket before breathing a sigh of relief as he scooped up a handful of condoms.

Soft, naked skin pressed against his side as Hanna leaned over him, stroking her fingers down his forearm to take one of the packages from him. "I'm glad you have extras."

Brad turned to her, shock diluting his brain power for a moment. "*You* have condoms?"

She hesitated. "I started carrying them a few days ago," she confessed.

He scooped her up and carried her back in front of the fire, tossing the extra supplies to one side before reheating the water and squeezing the washcloth clean.

Then he proceeded to enjoy himself thoroughly.

He washed her from head to toe, teasing as he pressed the warm cloth against her breasts, rubbing until her nipples were bright red and her chest shook with how hard she breathed.

He soaked the cloth again, pressing his hands against her thighs until she opened wider to let him stroke her pussy. Soft motions along each side of her labia followed, circling up and over her clit. Folding the cloth around his fingers so he could rub with precision until her hips rocked upward helplessly.

The heat from the fire poured forward, wrapping around them. Firelight brushed over her skin and highlighted her every motion. Brad put aside the cloth and picked her up, carried her to the bed, and laid her on the quilt-covered mattress.

Brad rested beside her, skimming a hand over her soft skin. "I want everything, all at the same time. I want to touch your breasts." He stroked his palm over her as he spoke. "I want to lick them until you're squirming. I want to nibble my way down between your legs then feast until you're calling my name. I need to be inside you."

Her fingers wrapped around his cock, and he sucked for air. "I need all that too. I want you, Brad."

No stopping now. He rolled, her slight body hot like a coal under him. She opened her legs wider and he settled closer. Braced on his elbows so he wouldn't crush her, he stared into her eyes.

"You've got me," he confessed. "All of me."

SHE'D SLIPPED into a happy dream, but one that wasn't out of reach. It was right there, happening to her. Her skin tingled where he'd touched her, which was pretty much everywhere. The clean scent of soap on his skin brought back memories of touching him intimately, of feeling his willingness to let her take control.

That moment was over though, as he brought their lips together and kissed—

Oh God, what a kiss. Hot and intense and shooting from need to urgency as if a thermometer had been pressed to the side of the stove.

As he kissed his way down her neck, Hanna closed her eyes and tried to calm her breathing, but it was no use. He seemed determined to devastate her. Pressing her breasts together so he could lick from one to the other more rapidly than she could control her breath. Nibbling on the tips he'd already made sensitive from the washcloth until she was ready to grab him by the ears and force him to make a move.

Then he was gone, settling between her legs, ready and willing to torment her all over in a brand-new way. He licked and touched and stroked. Teasing her clit, slipping his fingers inside her. A slow thrust, and another, but when he curled his fingers she just about hit the ceiling. She clutched the quilt as his touch sent an electric shock through her.

"What are you doing?" she demanded, elated and panicked all at the same time.

He just laughed and did it again, adding his tongue against her clit. There was no escape from the pleasure that roared up, exploding out as if she were one of those firecrackers that began with a single pop then burst in a dozen different directions, each one spiraling out of control with a screaming whistle.

She was still seeing stars as a condom wrapper crinkled. Then he was between her legs, the thick head of his cock against her. Easing in, pulling back.

She caught hold of his shoulders and stared into his face. His lashes fluttered a few times as he worked himself deeper, but it felt good. Oh, it felt so good, and when he finally stopped, fully buried in her, Hanna sighed, content.

"Finally."

His lips curled, and a soft laugh escaped as he held himself motionless. Present, so-completely present. She couldn't ignore that he was inside her, hard and broad and perfect.

Then he moved, and it only got better. "I'm going to lose my mind," he warned her in a whisper. "So damn good."

Hanna bent her knees farther, lifting them. He slipped even deeper. "More," she begged.

A groan escaped him as if she'd demanded the impossible, but then he sped up. Pressing deeper, thrusting harder. His shoulders and arm muscles bulging as she ran her fingers over them.

Touching was a connection. Joined—even more intimate.

He slid a hand over her belly and his fingers made contact with her clit, demanding a response. Pleasure spiraled higher as he pressed his mouth to hers, small pulses of his hips moving the head of his cock against the most sensitive part of her. His fingers shifted rapidly.

"*Brad.*" It took forever for her to say it because it took forever for her body to stop rocking, everything in her core coiling tight.

He gasped, lifting up and pressing deep. Brad buried himself over and over in a series of hard, frantic thrusts, pulling her orgasm out for an eternity until he froze, his cock jerking inside her, which set off another round of pleasure.

They were tangled up, legs and arms, lips moving together for a final desperate kiss before gasping for air.

He rolled her on top. Hanna's limbs were limp noodles as she pressed her ear to his chest to listen to the rapid thumping.

"That was amazing," she told him much later when she finally had the energy to speak.

"That was everything I've ever wanted," Brad said, before twirling her world upside down. He rolled them carefully until they lay side by side with him staring into her face as if he was trying to memorize her. "Hanna, sugar. *You're* everything I've ever wanted. There's something I need to ask—"

Out of the rafters over the bed, a small furry creature fell directly on Brad's head.

Smothering her amusement, Hanna sat, carefully scooping up the kitten that nuzzled against her, meowing piteously.

Brad laughed, rolling away and striding from the bed. She wasn't sure what all he did, but by the time she joined him at the table, placing Blackie carefully at the bowl of milk Brad had found, he didn't say anything more regarding whatever he'd been about to ask.

And she didn't remind him, but she *thought* she knew what he'd been about to ask, and the idea was both perfect, and perfectly terrifying.

That look in his eyes had been love. She was sure of it.

Throughout the day as he stoked the fire and they watched the storm rage against the windows, Hanna kept waiting for him to finish his question. Part of her kept hoping he wouldn't because she wasn't sure yet what her answer would be.

They played games and made meals and cuddled together until it became another session of lovemaking, and Hanna was just about one hundred percent sure what she would say when he did ask...

Which made the fact that he didn't all the more frustrating.

15

The cabin was still dark, and either Hanna had gone deaf and could no longer hear the wind howling past, or the storm had calmed. Her heart went back to fluttering the instant she came fully alert and realized where she was. In bed, with Brad.

Brad, who held her as if she were precious. His big arms cradled her tight then tugged until she was draped over him.

"Merry Christmas," Brad offered.

She wiggled—then froze as she realized the rock-solid bits of him included his cock, and she was right on top of it.

He brushed a finger over her cheek, that contented expression on his face that she was growing to enjoy far too much. "Such big eyes."

Three words. A new record. "You don't seem to be as grumpy as usual this morning," Hanna teased.

Brad raised a brow. "You're in my bed. That's better than coffee."

Hanna went for it, leaning in to kiss him, running her hands over him because she could. He groaned as she adjusted position, knees to either side of his body, her sex directly over his hard length. She undulated her hips a few times, and his breathing got faster. Tighter.

And when she leaned to the side and grabbed a condom, his smile widened.

Curses rang out—soft ones—as she slid his boxers down then went to cover him. Fumbling a little, working the edges of the condom over him with her hand until he caught her wrist in his and stopped her.

"*Hanna.*"

Begging. He was begging, and she was ready, and as she rose over him and guided him into her body, slowly, easing over his width, Hanna sighed with contentment.

Only once she was completely down, connected as one, did she lean forward. "Merry Christmas," she whispered.

She kissed him as she lifted and lowered. Brad caught her by the hips and helped, moving together until they were both breathless and somehow he was sitting up as well and she was wrapped tight in his arms.

They came staring into each other's eyes, and she was seconds away from telling him—

The wind rattled at the window, and they both glanced at the patch of sunshine on the floor. "I don't think the storm's done yet," Brad warned. "We'd better head home before we're trapped for the rest of the week."

She stroked a hand over his face. "Other than the fact we'd scare Crissy, that wouldn't be the worst disaster ever," she confessed.

His smile set in place and didn't vanish. Not as they cleaned up the cabin and packed up their things. They cleared off the sleds and headed out into the crisp, cold day. Sunshine sparkled blindingly bright against the piles of fresh powder.

It was exhilarating and wonderful, and in the midst of all of it, contentment rolled in, and Hanna knew.

She loved him. She trusted him, and when he did get around to asking, she was going to say yes, even though it might make no sense. They'd rushed forward so quickly after inching their way along the beginning of the relationship, but it seemed as if they were meant to be together.

He was the one she wanted. She wanted him for now and years into the future. She could just hear them in the future, talking about each other the way Patrick did about his wife, who'd been his other half.

They pulled into the barn, and Crissy came running, Patrick smiling behind her, leaning heavily on his canes.

Hanna held her little girl tight and kissed her. "Merry Christmas, sweetie."

"Merry Christmas, Mommy. We made breakfast, Mr. Patrick and I."

Crissy raced over to Brad to give him another hug and a kiss and to take Blackie from him, scolding the kitten as she carried it off to its mom.

"We've been fine," Patrick assured Hanna. "Now if you've got an appetite, Crissy made enough for a horde."

Everything seemed brighter as they walked into the kitchen. Crissy told them all about the stories Patrick had read the night before. How they'd waited for Santa to come down the chimney—

Brad lifted a hand and excused himself. "I'll be right back," he promised.

Hanna listened as her daughter shared excitedly. Brad passed by with a couple of brightly wrapped packages in his arms before returning to the kitchen where they ate themselves silly on pancakes, peaches and whipped cream.

Patrick stirred another spoon of sugar into his coffee. "My

belly is full to the brim. I guess it's time for a nap," he said, stretching his arms lazily in the air.

Crissy quivered in her chair, concern on her face.

"Yep, that's the best thing for a lazy Christmas morning." Patrick nodded at Hanna then winked where Crissy couldn't see it. "Can't think of another thing I'd rather do."

"We could open presents," Crissy suggested casually.

"But naps are nice," Hanna said with as straight a face as possible.

The fluttering in her belly became stronger as Brad exchanged glances with her before he spoke up. "Seriously? I have to agree with Crissy. I think we'd better open presents before nap time instead of after," he said.

"But you still think today should include nap time," Hanna teased.

His eyes flashed. "It's good to have a bit of a rest after a lot of excitement. I think we should all have a lie-down later today."

Her mouth went dry. *Okay, then.*

They gathered in the living room where the tree stood in the opposite corner to the fireplace, a small bundle of brightly wrapped packages at its base. Hanna recognized the couple that she and Crissy had picked up for Patrick and Brad, but there were a lot more.

Patrick motioned for Crissy to come forward. "Youngest person in the room is the elf," he decreed as he put a red Santa hat on her head.

She paused with her hands on his knees. "Okay. I'll be the helper this time."

Crissy scooped up a present and brought it to Brad, and they all watched as he unwrapped a new picture frame—a present from his father.

One after another they took turns unwrapping surprises. Patrick opened a small group of boxes that came from his friends that contained new tools to use in his workshop. Crissy opened a package from Patrick that held warm slippers and a robe. In the pocket was a stuffed toy rabbit wearing a matching outfit, and she laughed with childish delight and gave him a big hug.

The next present was delivered to Hanna. It took some work because the box was heavy, and Brad ended up helping Crissy drag it across the floor to Hanna's feet.

"It says *to the Lanes*," Crissy informed her. "That means you *and* me, right?"

"It does. Want to help me unwrap it?"

Silly question. Paper flew in all directions. Hanna glanced up to see Brad watching intently.

Crissy had the lid pried off an instant later. Her jaw dropped, mouth opening in a wide, comical gasp. "My books!"

Hanna leaned in closer to discover the top of the box held a layer of children's books, some paperback, some hardcover.

Familiar titles, all of them.

Crissy snatched up a book in either hand and jumped up and down excitedly. She whirled toward Hanna and shoved her hands forward. "There's *Andrew and the Wild Bikes*, and *The Secret World of Og*, and—" She laughed, digging into the box again as Hanna's heart filled with joy.

She glanced at Brad who was watching Crissy with delight. "Where did those—?"

"This isn't a book," Crissy interrupted, her face folding into a confused frown as she lifted away another layer of stories to reveal a sturdy plastic box.

Hanna opened the lid then lost her breath.

Inside were photographs. Pictures of Crissy as a baby—some in Hanna's arms, some not. Crissy as a toddler, often with other children. As Hanna flipped through there were images from every stage of life since they'd come to Heart Falls. Even a few from before—

Everything she'd thought completely gone, destroyed by the fire. All those bits of memory were right there in front of her.

It was her turn to stare slack-jawed at Brad. "How? How on earth?" Her throat closed off, and she swallowed hard, her breathing turning ragged.

"I asked around. Teachers, friends. Everyone who might've had a shot of either you or Crissy. Projects from school that asked for baby photos. All your friends went digging this past week and made copies. You have to do the work to put together a scrapbook, but now you've got the pictures to do it. And one of the pictures showed part of Crissy's bookshelf, so I blew it up and pulled the titles so I could order a few."

Crissy raced over to hug Brad fiercely before darting across the room to Patrick's side so he could admire her refound treasures.

Hanna's hands shook as she carefully placed the photo box aside, sliding from her chair and moving across the room to stand before Brad.

Maybe the days on the calendar said it was too quick, but she was without a single doubt. This man who'd been so careful and gentle with her and her daughter—he *cared*. He cared enough to help them find a bit of their past. The sweet memories that would've been hard to let go.

This was the man she wanted to walk beside into the future.

She stood beside him as she attempted to find the words. He waited patiently— Of course he did, because he was *Brad*, and he was exactly who she needed in her life.

His smile slowly widened. "I'm glad you like my gift."

"I love you." The words escaped because they were pounding through her very soul.

The room went quiet, Patrick and Crissy suddenly motionless in the background.

Brad's eyes fixed on hers.

She said it again, and this time it was easier and it felt even more right. "I love you. So much."

He pulled her into his arms and kissed her. Soft and tender, his arms cradling her. He pulled back just far enough to whisper against her cheek. "I'm glad, because I love you too."

She buried her face against his neck and took a deep breath, inhaling the scent of him. Feeling his strong arms around her.

She must've been high on Christmas fumes or something, because as shocking as it was to admit to him how she felt, she didn't stop there. "I don't want to be your girlfriend anymore," she said firmly.

He pushed her back and lifted her chin. "Ummm..."

"Crissy wants a daddy for Christmas, and I think Santa should deliver." Barely above a whisper, but very, very clear.

She'd expected him to look confused, or shocked, but what he did was tip his head back and laugh. A deep, happy sound that rolled up from deep inside before he grabbed hold and squeezed her tight.

He kissed her cheek and whispered against her ear. "I'd be proud to be Crissy's daddy, and very happy to be your husband."

He kissed her again, and all the hurts that had been tangled around her heart—the rejection and loneliness—burned away, leaving her pristine clean like the snow outside the remote cabin.

Shining with love.

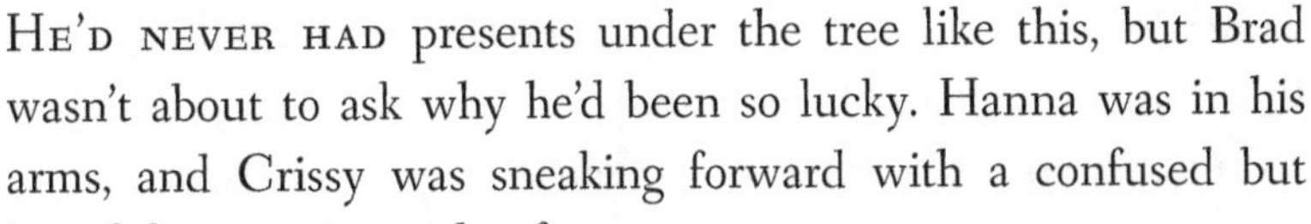

HE'D NEVER HAD presents under the tree like this, but Brad wasn't about to ask why he'd been so lucky. Hanna was in his arms, and Crissy was sneaking forward with a confused but hopeful expression on her face.

"Why's Mommy crying?"

Brad made room for Crissy to snuggle close. "Because she's happy."

"Oh." She eyed Brad's arms around Hanna, considered, then shrugged. "Okay."

Crissy crawled up on his knee so she could lean her head against Hanna's. "Don't cry, Mommy. It's Christmas."

Hanna raised a hand so she could stroke her daughter's hair. "I'm happy, sweetie, Brad's right. Sometimes when really good things happen, it makes tears come."

"Like being glad Blackie is safe?"

"Exactly like that," Brad told her. He glanced down at Hanna, waiting for permission to share their perfect news.

She stole a tissue from the box beside the chair, taking a deep breath before turning to her daughter. "We have something special to tell you."

Crissy tilted her head and waited.

Brad took a peek across the room at his father. Patrick had leaned back and was grinning in anticipation. There was no surprising that one.

"Your mommy and I are going to get married," he told Crissy. "Because I love her very much. And I love you too."

Her mouth hung open as she glanced from Hanna then back to him. "Seriously?" she demanded.

Hanna burst out laughing, delight dancing around the room like sparkling lights flickering off the shiny ornaments decorating the tree. "She already sounds like you," she teased Brad before answering her daughter. "Yes, *seriously*."

It took a while before all the hugs were finished, and there were a few more tears to wipe dry when Crissy suddenly realized this would make Patrick her grandpa.

Hanna got teary-eyed too as Patrick slipped an arm around her shoulders and held her tight, pressing a kiss against her temple.

They didn't have to say the words. Brad knew how much it meant for her to have an extended family again.

Eventually they moved the party into the kitchen to serve up slices of Patrick's cake. They were just about to sit down when the doorbell rang.

"I'll get it." Brad wondered who on earth would've dared the drive.

He opened the door to find his brother standing there, hat literally in one hand, the other holding a bag that held wrapped presents.

"You should slam the door on me, but I hope you won't," Mark said in a rush. "I know I'm stupid enough that I'll probably say the wrong thing at some point, but I want to stop fighting. I want my family back, and I'm ready to apologize."

Brad's head was spinning, but he backed up and gestured his brother in. "We're in the kitchen. Let me go warn Dad."

But Patrick already stood in the doorway, leaning heavily on his canes as he stared in shock at his oldest son.

Mark hesitated. "Merry Christmas, Dad."

Patrick's face crinkled with emotion then he nodded his head firmly. "Merry Christmas, Son."

He stood motionless for a moment before Mark stepped forward to give him a big hug, patting him on the shoulder before backing away with the pretense of organizing his gifts. "I brought a few things. Just trinkets, really, but I didn't want to show up empty-handed."

Brad paused, wondering if he should rush ahead to warn Hanna, but the chaos continued because she was there as well. Brad's jaw nearly hit the floor when she snuck around Patrick to offer Mark a hug.

Post-hug, his brother escaped into the kitchen as if he wasn't able to speak. Patrick followed, Crissy dancing between them, eager to be introduced to this new family member.

Brad caught Hanna by the wrist before she could disappear. "What just happened?" he demanded.

Hanna glanced over her shoulder into the kitchen then back at Brad. "It looks as if someone decided to put his head on straight."

"From the looks of things, I should ask if you were involved in his straightening up." He smiled as she tucked herself tighter against him, the pride on her face all too clear. "You, Hanna Lane, are one amazing woman."

"I'm going to be Hanna Ford," she reminded him. "We're engaged, right?"

"You definitely get my name. You've already got my heart," he told her before pointing overhead. "Oh, look, mistletoe."

She glanced up. "I don't see anything."

"Strange. I do."

Then he proceeded to kiss her the way he planned on kissing her for the next fifty years and more, whether there was mistletoe or not.

EPILOGUE

July, Lone Pine ranch, Heart Falls

Brooke Silver fought to keep her amusement under control as she watched her boyfriend Mack pound on the bathroom door again.

"Brad? You okay in there, dude?" Mack winked at her, and her amusement shifted to something warmer. Hotter.

His dark hair was cut neatly, and with his firm jawline and laughing eyes, Mack Klassen was already temptation personified. Dressed in a suit, he was too damn gorgeous.

The low groan of response from behind the door was slightly more reassuring than the silence they'd gotten the last two times Mack had attempted to pry the groom from where he'd vanished after turning an intriguing shade of green.

It appeared that while Mack's best friend Brad Ford could face down a fire without blinking, the idea of meeting his barely five-foot bride under the massive arbour constructed in the front yard of the Lone Pine ranch was more than the burly man could handle.

"Hanna is going be standing at the alter waiting for *him* if he doesn't hurry up," Brooke warned.

Mack snickered then pulled himself upright, all seriousness and firm determination, a glimpse of his military background shining through. "If Brad doesn't get his butt in gear, I have zero problem taking the door off its hinges and hauling him in front of the preacher over my shoulder."

"You'd look good as a delivery boy, but let's hope he gets there under his own power." Brooke took one final satisfying glance up and down his suit be-decked muscular body then smiled approvingly. "Well, I'll leave you to your entertainment. I need to go make sure the bride isn't having second thoughts."

"Tell her I've got everything under control," Mack said.

She hurried down the hallway, her modestly high heels clicking against the wood floor as she made her way to the bedroom where Hanna was doing final preparation for the big moment. Hanna wasn't planning on running away—she was so in love with her big firefighter it glowed out of her.

Brooke slipped into the bedroom to discover Hanna had moved to a stool low enough her daughter Crissy could poke tiny white flowers into the braid wrapped around her head.

Hanna lifted her gaze but kept motionless. "Everything okay?"

It was the perfect moment for Brooke to lie her ass off. "Everything's great, and *you* are beautiful."

That last part wasn't a lie. Hanna was a vision, her outfit not quite a white wedding gown, but more than a simple sundress. It was something Hanna said she'd be able to wear over and over to remind her of this day, and Brooke thought that was one of the sweetest things she'd ever heard.

Crissy finished placing the last of the teeny blossoms in her mother's hair. She stepped back and raised her hand to her mouth, tears filling her eyes. "You look like a princess, Mommy."

Hanna pulled her daughter into her arms, strategically shutting down what looked to be the onset of tears. "Thank you, sweetie." She kissed her little girl. "Now let's go with Brooke so we can finish getting your basket ready. Then we can go outside. It should be almost time to meet your daddy."

Crissy glanced up at Brooke. "I get to call him Daddy because he loves me."

"It's a wonderful thing to have a daddy who loves you," Brooke responded seriously.

She held out her hand and led Crissy to the kitchen. She took a quick glance down the hallway, thankful to see Mack was no longer lounging outside the bathroom door. It appeared the crisis had been averted.

They finished putting the final few roses in the small silver bucket that Crissy held right before another of their friends opened the door a crack and whispered "It's time!"

Brooke glanced at Hanna to make sure she was ready.

More than ready from the happiness shining on her face as she held her daughter's hand and nodded at Brooke.

Showtime.

Brooke led the way to the grassy path where family and friends were gathered under the apple tree. Low chairs rested on either side of the center aisle. Everyone remained seated as Brooke stepped aside and walked around the gathering to join Mack at the edge of the congregation.

Brad waited at the front, right beside the strong tree trunk. His gaze fixed on Hanna and Crissy, his smile showing no indication of his earlier nerves. There was nothing there but anticipation and love.

At Brooke's side, Mack slipped his hand around hers and held on.

Watching her friend fall in love had been amazing, and now

getting to witness her and Brad make a lifetime commitment to each other was extra special.

Standing in witness with Mack at her side—even better. Brooke stole a glance at him but quickly looked back to where Brad had taken one of Hanna's hands in his, and they'd turned to face the preacher to make their public vows.

Did she want this for herself? Possibly, but there was no need to rush. If someday she and Mack were ready for more, then the next thing would happen. Brooke was pretty firm believer that everything would work out at the right time—she'd built up enough good karma over the years to let fate take care of her.

Today was for cheering for Brad and Hanna, and little Crissy who had a daddy who loved her. Brooke leaned tighter against Mack's side and trusted that eventually the future would arrive.

~

November, Calgary

MACK WHISTLED LAZILY as he wandered out of the sporting goods shop and into the mall. His mission to pick up the required items for the fire hall training sessions was complete. Now he had time to kill until the other guys were done their shopping. He turned the corner and came to a complete halt, his gaze fixed on an enormous picture of Brooke plastered on the wall. Her light brown hair with blonde highlights was tousled beautifully over her shoulders, and she was gazing with adoration at a dark-haired man just visible at the edge of the poster.

What the hell?

His heart rate shot up. He might have been in in the middle of a mission or called out to deal with a fire, the adrenaline rush hit so hard. That was *his* Brooke—

Upon closer examination it became clear the woman was

very similar to but *not* his girlfriend. It took a little while for the surge of anger and confusion to fade.

It took another moment to gather the courage to admit the reason he felt so unsettled was because Brooke wasn't supposed to look at another man like that.

They hadn't officially made their relationship anything more than steady dating, and there were good reasons for that, but he'd known for a while it was time to take the next step. He loved being with her, loved every bit of time they spent together. She made him laugh, and she listened, and the fact that he now stood outside of a jewelry store that was advertising engagement rings modelled by a woman who looked almost exactly like Brooke—

Karma was playing games with him.

He peeled his gaze off the poster and continued down the mall, deliberately pushing aside the moment of jealousy and instead dwelling on the truth he had realized. It was time to do the next thing.

He needed to propose, but it needed to be something beyond just taking her out to dinner and passing her a ring. Even going down on one knee didn't seem like it was a memorable enough event—

Curses muttered under his breath as he confronted another image of Brooke. A second jewelry store, and another huge promotion featuring a woman who looked enough like her at first glance he could've sworn it was her, arms wrapped around another man's neck.

It wasn't good that he instantly imagined his *hands* wrapped around the other man's neck. Brooke would not appreciate Mack's caveman thoughts, and he needed to get them under control, stat.

This time he moved a little closer, though. Peered in the window of the shop and glanced at the ring display. It wasn't the price tags that made him turn away, it was the fact the rings all looked the same.

Pretty, he supposed, and shiny, but none of them good enough for his Brooke.

By the time he'd reached the end of the mall and had two more experiences with coming face to face with engagement rings sales and promotional material that set his blood pounding, Mack had decided that karma was no longer playing nice. She was bound and determined he be prepared to propose.

He was equally determined to stick to his guns. As pretty as the rings were, unless Brooke picked it out from behind the counter herself, he was not about to purchase one of the generic stock.

But the sooner he got out of the mall, the better. Escape the stores, and karma would be temporarily defeated.

His teammates returned, and the three of them got back in the truck and headed down the highway, returning to Heart Falls.

"Shoot—Mack, can you pull over by the hardware store there?" Alex pointed off the side of the main road. "Forgot I needed to pick up a few things for Silver Stone."

"No problem."

While the other two men disappeared into the hardware store, Mack drifted into the thrift shop next door. It was a smaller size place, one of those community-based and family-run shops. The long-haired gentleman behind the till smiled encouragingly as Mack found some used T-shirts to wear when he had dirty tasks to do around the fire hall.

He was paying for his purchases when karma, that determined bitch, decided to take absolute control of his life.

What came next was an experience that he looked forward to sharing with Brooke—after he'd proposed and she'd said yes.

Because, beyond any logic or reason, karma won.

As he stood outside the building and stared down at the ring resting in his palm—the ring he'd purchased because it was absolutely perfect for Brooke—all he knew for certain was that sometime in the next while he had one important task.

Find the most memorable way possible to ask Brooke to be his forever.

~

New York Times Bestselling Author Vivian Arend invites you to Heart Falls. These contemporary ranchers live in a tiny town in central Alberta, tucked into the rolling foothills. Enjoy the ride as they each find their happily-ever-afters.

~

The Stones of Heart Falls
A Rancher's Heart
A Rancher's Song
A Rancher's Bride
A Rancher's Love
A Rancher's Vow

~

Holidays at Heart Falls
A Firefighter's Christmas Gift
A Soldier's Christmas Wish
A Hero's Christmas Hope
A Cowboy's Christmas List
A Rancher's Christmas Kiss

~

The Colemans of Heart Falls
The Cowgirl's Forever Love
The Cowgirl's Secret Love
The Cowgirl's Chosen Love

ABOUT THE AUTHOR

With over 2.5 million books sold, Vivian Arend is a *New York Times* and *USA Today* bestselling author of over 60 contemporary and paranormal romance books, including the Six Pack Ranch and Granite Lake Wolves.

Her books are all standalone reads with no cliffhangers. They're humorous yet emotional, with sexy-times and happily-ever-afters. Vivian pretty much thinks she's got the best job in the world, and she's looking forward to giving readers more HEAs. She lives in B.C. Canada with her husband of many years and a fluffy attack Shih-tzu named Luna who ignores everyone except when treats are deployed.

www.vivianarend.com